AMISH ROMANCE

AMISH BED AND BREAKFAST, BOOK 4

RUTH HARTZLER

Amish

ROMANCE BOOKS

GLOSSARY

Pennsylvania Dutch is a dialect. It is often written as it sounds, which is why you will see the same word written several different ways. The word 'Dutch' has nothing to do with Holland, but rather is likely a corruption of the German word 'Deitsch' or 'Deutsch'.

Glossary

ab im kopp - addled in the head
Ach! (also, *Ack!*) - Oh!
aenti - aunt
appeditlich - delicious
Ausbund - Amish hymn book
bedauerlich - sad

bloobier - blueberry

boppli - baby

bopplin - babies

bro - bread

bruder(s) - brother(s)

bu - boy

Budget, The - weekly newspaper for Amish and Mennonite communities. Based on Sugarcreek, Ohio, and has 2 versions, Local and National.

buwe - boys

daag - day

Daed, Datt, Dat (vocative) - Dad

Diary, The - Lancaster County based Amish newspaper. Focus is on Old Order Amish.

Dawdi (also, *Daadi*) (vocative) - Grandfather

dawdi haus (also, *daadi haus, grossdawdi haus*) - grandfather's or grandparents' house (often a small house behind the main house)

de Bo - boyfriend

Die Botschaft - Amish weekly newspaper. Based in PA but its focus is nation-wide.

demut - humility

denki (or *danki*) - thank you

Der Herr - The Lord

dochder - daughter

dokter - doctor

doplich - clumsy

dumm - dumb

dummkopf - idiot, dummy

Dutch Blitz - Amish card game

English (or *Englisch*) (adjective) - A non-Amish person

Englischer (noun) - A non-Amish person

familye - family

ferhoodled - foolish, crazy

fraa - wife, woman

froh - happy

freind - friend

freinden - friends

gegisch - silly

geh - go

gern gheschen (also, gern *gschehne*) - you're welcome

Gott (also, *Gotte*) - God

grank - sick, ill

grossboppli - grandbaby

grossdawdi (also, *dawdi, daadi haus, gross dawdi)* - grandfather, or, in some communities, great grandfather

grosskinskind - great-grandchild

grosskinskinner - great-grandchildren

grossmammi (or *grossmudder*) - grandmother

gross-sohn - grandson

grossvadder - grandfather (see also *grossdawdi*)

gude mariye - good morning

guten nacht (also, *gut nacht*) - good night

gude nochmiddaag - good afternoon

gut - good

haus - house

Herr - Mr.

Hiya - Hi

hochmut - pride

Hullo (also, *Hallo*) - Hello

hungerich - hungry

Ich liebe dich - I love you

jah (also *ya*) - yes

kaffi (also, *kaffee*) - coffee

kapp - prayer covering worn by women

kichli - cookie

kichlin - cookies

kinn (also, *kind*) - child

kinner - children

kinskinner - Grandchildren

Kumme (or *Kumm*) - Come

lieb - love, sweetheart

liewe - a term of endearment, dear, love

liede - song

maid (also, *maed*) - girls

maidel (also, *maedel*) - girl

Mamm (also, *Mammi*) - Mother, Mom

Mammi - Grandmother

mann - man

mariye-esse - breakfast

mei - my

meidung - shunning

mei lieb - my love

mein liewe - my dear, my love

menner - men

mudder - mother

naerfich - nervous

naut (also, *nacht*) - night

nee (also *nein*) - no

nix - nothing

nohma - name

onkel - uncle

Ordnung - "Order", the unwritten Amish set of rules, different in each community

piffle (also, *piddle*) - to waste time or kill time

Plain - referring to the Amish way of life

rett (also, *redd*) - to put (items) away or to clean up.

rootsh (also, *ruch*) - not being able to sit still.

rumspringa (also, *rumschpringe*) - Running around years - when Amish youth (usually around the age of sixteen) leave the community for time and can be

English, and decide whether to commit to the Amish way of life and be baptized.

schatzi - honey

schee - pretty, handsome

schecklich - scary

schmaert - smart

schtupp - family room

schweschder - sister

schweschdern - sisters

schwoger - brother-in-law

seltsam - strange, unnatural

sohn - son

vadder - father

verboten - forbidden

Vorsinger - Song leader

was its let - what is the matter?

wie gehts - how are you?

wilkum (also, *wilkom*) - welcome

wunderbar (also, *wunderbaar*) - wonderful

yer - you

yourself - yourself

youngie (also, *young*) - the youth

yung - young

CHAPTER 1

*M*iriam woke with a crick in her neck. She had not slept well the night before, and her heart felt heavy. She wasn't sure why, only that Jonas had come to her in a dream, his kind eyes smiling at her. After she rose, she washed and dressed. Outside morning dawned, but a thick mist made its way through the beautiful farming community. She folded some bread in a napkin and decided to walk down to the pond, to sit among the ducks and the whispering reeds.

Miriam stepped into the cool morning air and stretched out her arms, watching as the sunlight played on the trees. She walked down to the gate and waved to a married couple in a buggy making their way up the road. There was a pang in her heart. As a widow, she missed the happy times with her husband. She missed having someone around, and her loneliness seemed to swallow her whole, like it was a cloud.

Returning inside, she collected her coat and then stepped outside again, to walk down to the large pond where a little family of ducks lived. She did not want to be in Eden right now, remembering her old *haus* in Ohio where her husband used to hang his coat and his hat, and the place where she would set down their food at the end of a long day of hard work.

The ground crunched underfoot as Miriam walked. She could hear the *menner* in the nearby fields, and for a moment she paused to reflect upon her somber mood. Finally arriving at the pond, she stood and watched the rippling water.

When Miriam had lost her husband, she had not just lost him, but the life they were going to have. She could feel the children she dreamed of having with him in her arms. She could smell them and kiss them and sing to them, but of course this was all in her dreams, because her husband had died before they ever had the chance to start the big *familye* she had always wanted. Rachel was her only child, and now Rachel was married to Isaac and had a *boppli* of her own.

Miriam had planned on being alone by the lake, but when she looked back at Eden, she noticed a figure on her roof silhouetted against the rising sun. It was Jonas. Miriam was going to call out and wave, but Jonas looked so lost in thought as he stood there and looked over the fields, that she hated to rouse him from his own mind. Jonas really was such a handsome man with broad, strong shoulders and a kind heart.

For a long time Miriam watched Jonas work on the roof, as the day grew brighter and brighter.

Returning to Eden, Miriam took off her coat and looked around. After a minute, she went to her room to find the box where she kept all the letters she had once written to her husband, and the letters he had written back. Taking one out of the bundle, she rubbed the paper between her hands. There was something about the texture of the letter, and something about seeing her late husband's neat handwriting scribbled over the paper, that made her heart feel terribly heavy and sad.

She put away the letters and thought of Jonas.

He really did have the kindest eyes. Still, there was no time to think upon her own concerns, because Eden was about to have a fresh influx of guests.

CHAPTER 2

*M*iriam was a little concerned that all the new guests were arriving at once. This hadn't happened before. Usually, one person left, and then another person arrived, but today, several new guests were coming at the same time.

Miriam was grateful that Tiffany was there to help her. Tiffany had become a hard worker, and while she was still becoming accustomed to the Amish ways, and from time to time complained incessantly, she was nevertheless a great help and Miriam had come to rely on her.

The first guest to arrive was Jake Reeves, a young man with sharp, pointed features and nervous eyes that darted from side to side. Jake had told Miriam when booking that he was an author, coming to lock himself into his room to finish a novel he had been working on for a year and a half. With that in mind, Miriam had decided to put him in the room with the best view of the creek.

Miriam gave Jake a reassuring smile, but he avoided eye contact. Miriam wondered if he was normally so shy and uncomfortable around people, and so brooding and intense, or whether he had simply not encountered an Amish person before. Miriam was well aware that the Amish often made *Englischers* uncomfortable, simply because they were different.

"I have a lovely room for you, Mr. Reeves," Miriam said. "It has a beautiful view of the creek."

"Authors aren't like what you see in Hollywood movies," Jake snapped. "They don't stare at beautiful scenery waiting for inspiration to strike. They have to work hard. It's not as glamorous as it's made out to be."

Miriam merely nodded. She would have loved to say that she had never seen a Hollywood movie, and likewise had no idea of what was or was not glamorous, but she held her tongue. "If you'll follow me, Mr. Reeves, I'll show you to your room," was all she said.

Just then, an elderly lady bustled through the door clutching a hairy dog under her arm. "Is this Eden?" the woman said, her cheeks flushed. "Please tell me I don't have the wrong place! I couldn't stand it if I had the wrong place. That would upset me greatly."

Miriam rubbed her forehead. "Tiffany, would you please show Mr. Reeves to his room? I'll see to this lady."

Tiffany did as she was asked and then Miriam approached the lady. She was heavily made up and seemed a little eccentric, but had a sweet look on her face. "Are you Mrs. Ava Douglas?" Miriam asked her.

An unmistakable look of relief flashed across the woman's face. "Yes, I am, and this is Cuddles. He's a Pomeranian." She shoved the dog at Miriam, who took a step backward.

"Does he bite?" Miriam asked tentatively, looking at a protruding set of bottom teeth.

Mrs. Douglas laughed. "No, don't let his looks scare you. I got him cheaply because something went wrong with him. He was supposed to be a show dog, but as you can see, he isn't." She burst into laughter. "Go on, pat him," she urged Miriam.

Miriam stretched out her hand, hoping her fingers weren't about to be bitten, but the little dog seemed accepting of her attention. Miriam wasn't used to little dogs like this—her father always said any animal must be worth its keep. The cats she had growing up were to kill mice, and the only dogs were working dogs, not pets. Still, Miriam had always wanted a pet, but had never had the time to look after one.

"I'll show you to your room, Mrs. Douglas," Miriam began, but the lady interrupted her.

"Please, call me Ava."

"Ava." Miriam shot the woman a warm smile. "I've put you on the ground floor, because you said you're not very mobile."

"Yes, it's my arthritis," Ava said. "I have to have a hip replacement soon, maybe even knee replacements and a shoulder replacement."

Miriam looked at the woman appraisingly. She looked quite fit and trim, but Miriam knew that appearances could be deceptive. One of the ladies back home in Ohio had been quite thin prior to her hip replacement, and had then put on weight. That lady had told Miriam that the pain had made her thin. Miriam's heart went out to Ava. "Well, Ava, please call me Miriam. I'll show you to your room, and I hope you and Cuddles will be happy there."

Ava thanked her. "Cuddles sleeps all day and night. You won't hear a word out of him. I've left my bags in the car—would you please send a man for them?"

Miriam smiled to herself. "Sure, I'll have your bags to you in no time." She was used to *Englischers* thinking she wasn't strong, yet all her years of working on the farm back in Ohio had made her as strong as many *Englischer* men, she figured.

Ava exclaimed with delight when she saw her room. Miriam was pleased that Ava liked it, as it was a plain room, and *Englischers* often expected something fancy. Still, she had advertised Eden as a place where guests could experience the Amish way of life.

A quilt chest stood under the window, opposite a hickory rocking chair. An oak closet was in the corner. This was for the benefit of guests, as most *Englischers* did not like to hang their clothes from pegs on the wall. The plain walls contrasted with that of the brightly colored Lone Star quilt on the double bed, its brilliant orange, red, and yellow standing out against the midnight blue background.

Ava was clearly delighted that Miriam had gone to the trouble to provide a little dog bed. "Cuddles is crate trained," Ava said. "He always sleeps in his crate at night. That's the way the breeder trained him and he finds security in there. I leave the door open for him, but he sleeps in his crate. Still, it's so kind of you to put that little dog bed in there for him."

"I'll just get your bags for you," Miriam said with a smile. She took a deep breath as she walked to the car. Ava seemed lovely, but she hoped Jake wouldn't be a problem.

Miriam had so much trouble with people looking for the reported treasure in the grounds of Eden in the past, but she hoped those troubles were now behind her. The townsfolk were convinced that Captain Kidd's treasure was buried either under Eden itself, or in the nearby fields. Eden was named after Dr. John Eden. John Eden was one of Captain Kidd's men who retired to Pennsylvania, taking with him plenty of gold. Eden, Miriam's house, was said to stand on the site of John Eden's original house. No one had ever found any of the lost gold, but that hadn't stopped treasure hunters looking for it.

Miriam also hoped that the next two groups of

guests would not arrive at the same time, but judging by the two cars heading her way, she realized those hopes were in vain. Happily, Jonas appeared at her shoulder. "It looks like you're overrun by guests," he said with a chuckle.

"Yes, but it's something I'm grateful for. Still, it would be good if they didn't all arrive at once," Miriam added. She hoped Jonas would stay around and help her, and to her relief, he showed no sign of going.

Both expected couples were newly married and on vacation. The first couple appeared to have just had an argument, given their manner to each other. They were decidedly icy, but they were also somewhat icy to Miriam and Jonas. They introduced themselves as Bruce and Heather Hanson. Jonas offered to carry their bags upstairs to their room.

The Hansons were only halfway to the door when the last guests arrived. By process of elimination, Miriam knew these would be Kevin and Susan Smith. The two of them took a long time to get out of their car, because they were kissing. When they finally did get out of the car, they clung to each other and kissed again, before acknowledging Miriam's presence.

Tiffany appeared beside Miriam, startling her. "Quite a PDA," she said.

"What's a PDA?" Miriam whispered.

Tiffany chuckled. "Public display of affection. It looks like we have some interesting guests."

Miriam sighed. That certainly seemed to be the truth.

CHAPTER 3

*M*iriam was preparing breakfast for the guests, when Tiffany raced into the room. "It's the sheriff!" she shrieked.

Miriam frowned. *Whatever could the sheriff want?* she wondered. Miriam hurried to the front door, Tiffany on her heels. She flung the door open to see flashing red and blue lights on the vehicle outside.

"Sorry to disturb you again, Mrs. Berkholder," the sheriff said, "but there's been an incident in town. One of the jewelry stores was robbed last night. The funny thing is, only one diamond necklace was stolen. It wasn't a valuable necklace, and the thief ignored far more valuable pieces of jewelry." He scratched his head. "What's even stranger is that the thief climbed up a drainpipe. Someone would have to be agile to do that."

"But what does that have to do with me?" Miriam asked, puzzled. "Please don't tell me this has anything to do with Captain Kidd's treasure."

The sheriff wiped a weary hand across his brow. "I certainly hope not this time, for your sake, Mrs. Berkholder." He rubbed his chin. "No, it seems unrelated."

Miriam frowned. "So then why did you call by to tell me?"

The sheriff hesitated and looked at Tiffany. "Miss Bedshill, can you tell me the whereabouts of your car?"

Tiffany pointed to the barn. "It's next to the barn. You can see it clearly from here. Why?"

The sheriff wasted no time in coming to the point. "A car matching the description of your car and with your plates was seen speeding away from the jewelry store in the middle of the night, just after the time the crime was perpetrated."

Tiffany's face went white. "But, but…" she sputtered. "I haven't driven it for ages, not since I turned Amish!"

The sheriff crossed his arms over his chest. "So why do you still own the car?"

Tiffany shook her head in obvious frustration. "My parents were angry that I joined the community. I took the car back to them and left it there when I broke the news to them. We had an awful row, so I took a cab home. Anyway, about five or so days later, they sent the car back to me."

"Why?"

Tiffany shrugged, and wiped a tear from her eye. "I haven't spoken to them since we had the big row. They sent people who work for them to bring the car back to me. I asked them why, but they didn't know. I didn't know what to do with the car, so Mrs. Berkholder said I could leave it here."

"And where are the keys to your vehicle?"

Tiffany looked at Miriam. "I keep the keys," Miriam said.

"And they would be whereabouts now?" the sheriff asked. "Mrs. Berkholder, could you please see if you still have the keys?"

Miriam nodded. She went back into the house with Tiffany and the sheriff following her. She went into the kitchen and opened the top drawer to the old oak dresser. The keys were gone. Miriam spread around the contents of the drawer, but it was apparent that the keys weren't there. She turned to the sheriff. "The keys are missing."

"Who knew the keys were there?" the sheriff asked her.

Miriam thought for a moment. "Well, it wasn't a secret." She shrugged. "I mean, everyone knew. Jonas knew, and his workers James and Ethan did, too. My daughter, Rachel, probably knew and of course Tiffany knew. I don't expect any of the guests knew, because I haven't seen any of the guests in the kitchen yet. Oh, I almost forgot. Mrs. Douglas came to the kitchen last night with Heather Hanson and Susan Smith to ask for Advil. The Advil was in the same drawer as the keys, so any of the women could have seen the keys."

The sheriff appeared to be thinking this over. "Would you mind having a look around to see if anything else is missing or if anything is out of place?"

Oh no, it's happening again, was all Miriam could think. It was bad enough that Captain Kidd's treasure had interrupted her life ever since she arrived at Eden, but now there was a jewelry robbery in town, and it was in some way connected with her Bed and Breakfast establishment. What was she to do?

Upon reflection, Miriam realized there was nothing she *could* do. She searched the kitchen and the office, but could find nothing untoward. "That's the only strange thing I can find," she said to the sheriff upon her return.

"And you didn't take the car out last night?" he asked Tiffany.

Tiffany's face changed from ashen to pale green. "No, I certainly didn't. I told you, I haven't driven the car since I joined the community. You can ask around."

The sheriff held up his hands. "Now, miss, I'm not accusing anyone. I'm just trying to get the facts straight. Mrs. Berkholder, by the number of cars outside, I assume you have several guests?" Miriam nodded, but before she could respond, he pushed on. "I need to see your register, please, and I will need to speak to each of the guests."

"They'll all be down for breakfast soon," Miriam said in a small voice. She didn't think that being interrogated by the sheriff before breakfast would endear anyone to her B&B.

Miriam and Tiffany stayed in the kitchen while the sheriff questioned each guest in turn. The sheriff then went to look at Tiffany's car and found the keys in it. He bagged them.

When the sheriff drove away, Miriam and Tiffany served breakfast to the guests in the dining room. "Please accept my apologies for the police intrusion," Miriam said, eyeing the guests warily.

"Oh, it's all a bit of excitement, isn't it, dear," Ava Douglas said excitedly. "I can't wait to tell Cuddles. The two of us usually have such a boring life, but now there's been a bank robbery real close to us!"

"It was a jewelry theft, actually," Kevin Smith pointed out.

Ava tittered. "Oh dearie me, was it? Oh well, that's even more exciting, isn't it! Do you think it was a cat burglar? The sheriff said the thief climbed up a drainpipe."

"What was that old movie with a cat burglar?" Susan Smith asked. "Was it Rock Hudson or Jimmy Stewart?"

Her question was met with blank faces, but Ava spoke up. "It was Cary Grant, of course."

"Jake Reeves isn't here," Miriam said to Tiffany, when the guests were happily discussing old Hollywood movies that Miriam knew nothing about.

"I saw the sheriff questioning him not too long ago," Kevin piped up. "Maybe he's gone back to his room."

Miriam nodded. "Tiffany, would you please

knock on Mr. Reeves' door and tell him that breakfast is ready?"

While Tiffany was away, the guests excitedly discussed the robbery. "Did the sheriff say how much was stolen?" Heather Hansen asked. "Would it be worth billions? Thousands? Will it be on the news later?"

Miriam was at a loss how to respond, when Tiffany returned. "There's a *Do Not Disturb* sign hanging on his door."

Miriam nodded. "Tiffany, we'll keep some scrapple warm for him."

Miriam and Tiffany always ate breakfast with the guests. The guests came to Eden Bed and Breakfast to have a full Amish experience, and Miriam was amazed at the way in which Tiffany's website had brought in more guests. The girl truly was a blessing from *Gott*, even though she seemed to be the exact opposite when she had arrived. It was true that *Gott* works in mysterious ways.

When Miriam and Tiffany returned with cereal and fruit to finish the breakfast meal, Jake was sitting at the table. "Mr. Reeves," Miriam said, "I'll just get you some warm food."

Jake looked around the table. "Have I missed something?"

"We're just finishing breakfast," Kevin Smith told him.

Jake looked confused. "So why are you serving cereal and fruit now?" His comment was addressed to Miriam.

"In our community, we often finish breakfast with cereal, fruit and milk," Miriam explained. "I can't say that's the same for Amish everywhere, because every community will do things somewhat differently. It *is* the case in our community, however. Would you like me to fetch you your hot breakfast?"

"No thanks." Jake nearly spat the words. "I couldn't sleep last night, not with all the noise. I'll just have coffee, thanks."

"What noise was that?" Miriam asked him, puzzled.

"Well, the noise didn't last long. I thought I heard someone outside my window making noises in the bushes and then I heard the noise again a few hours later."

Miriam thought on what Jake said. Jake's room was directly above Ava's room. "Did you hear any noise, Mrs. Douglas?" she asked her.

"Please call me Ava," she said. "No, I didn't, but then I sleep like a rock. Why, the devil himself wouldn't be able to wake me once I'm in a deep sleep." She looked from Miriam to Tiffany and then back again at Miriam. "Oh, I mean no offense."

Miriam was puzzled. "I'm not sure what you mean."

"By mentioning the devil. I hope that didn't offend you." Before Miriam could respond, she pushed on. "Isn't it exciting, all of us being suspects in the bank robbery?"

This time nobody pointed out that it had been a jewelry robbery and not a bank robbery. Miriam was beginning to think that Ava Douglas was a little eccentric. "Did anyone else hear noises outside last night?"

Bruce and Heather, and Kevin and Susan shook their heads.

Miriam bit her lip. The four of them were on the other side of the house to Jake and Ava. Clearly, someone had broken into Eden and stolen Tiffany's keys. But how did they know the keys were there? It just didn't make any sense.

CHAPTER 4

*M*iriam had gotten into the habit of having two dinners a week for all the guests. Tonight she was going to serve chicken pot pie. Miriam checked the chicken and found it had cooked nicely, so she added potatoes along with some celery and carrots to simmer for an hour.

She was adjusting her apron when Jake came in. "Is that girl still working?" he asked abruptly.

"Do you mean Tiffany?" Miriam asked him.

He nodded.

"Is there something you would like?"

He nodded again. "I get very hot at night and sweat, so I'd like more linen in my room, please."

"Sure, I'll fetch Tiffany. Is now a suitable time?"

"Yes, it is. I just wanted to walk around the grounds. That is, if you have no objection?"

"Of course not. Please feel free to enjoy the pond, and the gazebo." Jake left, and Miriam found Tiffany polishing a large mahogany cabinet in the sitting room. "Tiffany, Mr. Reeves wants more sheets taken to his room. Would you do that?"

Tiffany looked relieved to be doing anything other than polishing. *At least she's not pretending to be allergic to polish now*, Miriam thought, as she returned to her meal preparation.

Miriam turned her attention to making pot pie noodles. She made a hole in a cup of flour and dropped the egg in, and then stirred it with a fork. She added a pinch of baking soda and half a teaspoon of salt and then carefully added the right amount of milk to make firm dough. Miriam was rolling the dough thin when Tiffany returned.

"I think Jake Reeves is the thief!" Tiffany said, rather too loudly.

"Hush!" Miriam held her finger to her mouth. "Someone might hear you. Why do you say that?"

"Because he has diamond earrings in his room!"

Miriam cut the dough into squares. "Tiffany, that doesn't mean he's a thief. They are likely his earrings."

"I don't think they'd suit him," Tiffany said with a laugh.

Miriam shook her head. "Tiffany, you know what I meant, that he owns those earrings. Perhaps they're a gift for his mother, or his girlfriend. Besides, if he was a thief, he'd hardly leave his ill gotten gains out on display."

Tiffany shook her head. "That's just it—they weren't out on display." She stopped speaking for a moment, and her cheeks flushed red. "I wasn't snooping, truly I wasn't. It's just that I carried in sheets and didn't see he had a bag in front of me so I tripped over it and fell hard." She pulled down a sleeve and pointed to her grazed elbow. "See! Anyway, I tripped over his bag and the earrings fell out. Do you think we should tell the sheriff?"

Miriam bit her lip. That was a good question. Should she tell the sheriff? She didn't want the sheriff to come and frighten her guests away, but then again, what if Jake was indeed the thief?

Miriam was deep in thought, but looked up to see Tiffany hopping from one foot to the other. "What is it, Tiffany?" she asked. "Was there something else?"

Tiffany nodded. "You know the newlyweds, Kevin and Susan Smith? Well, when I cleaned their room this morning, I noticed that the couch in their room was made up."

Miriam was puzzled. "What do you mean that it was made up?"

Tiffany clasped her hands. "I mean, you know, *made up* as if someone was sleeping on it overnight."

Miriam tapped her chin. "That's a little strange, but perhaps they had an argument. Anyway, Tiffany, we mustn't breach our guests' privacy. Whatever they do is their own concern, and it's not for us to comment on it."

Tiffany was not deterred. "But don't you see! What if they're only posing as a married couple in order to hide their clandestine activities! They could be the jewelry thieves and they're only pretending to be a married couple. You saw how they were all over each other yesterday, and now they're sleeping apart? Newlyweds? Something just doesn't add up."

Miriam shook her head. "Maybe not, but we still shouldn't pry, Tiffany. Now don't you have some polishing to do?"

Tiffany went back to her polishing with a skip in her step. Miriam smiled to herself. Tiffany had not long been in the community, so Miriam suspected she was looking for excitement. Miriam had never been anything but Amish, but she figured that anyone who had left the *Englisch* world and joined the community would have to find it quite difficult at first and not as eventful as their old life.

Still, was Tiffany right? Someone had taken Tiffany's car and robbed a jewelry store. It only stood to reason that it was one of the guests. And now there were diamonds in Jake's room, and not only that, but the very affectionate newlyweds appeared to be sleeping apart. Was there something going on? It seemed that there was. "Wu schmoke is, is aa feier," Miriam said aloud. *Where there's smoke, there's fire.*

Miriam spun around at the sound of someone clearing their throat. "Jonas! You startled me!"

Jonas smiled. "You were miles away, Miriam. What did you mean by your comment?"

"No, I don't like to gossip, Jonas."

Jonas frowned so deeply that cracks formed around his eyes. "Something is troubling you, Miriam, and the sheriff is concerned about the guests. Maybe you should tell me what's going on. It's not gossip; it's a conversation between two *gut* friends."

Miriam nearly said, 'Is that what we are, *gut* friends?' but she caught herself in time. Jonas was not dating another woman, but he wasn't dating her, either. She at times was certain there was something between them, or was it simply wishful thinking on her part? Were her feelings for him truly not reciprocated? Did he really only see her as a *gut* friend? Was his kindness toward her simply the kindness anyone from within the community would show to another? The only way by which she would find out for sure would be to ask Jonas, and there was no way she was going to do that. Miriam looked up to see Jonas staring at her, clearly waiting for an answer. "It might be nothing…" Her voice trailed away.

"But?" Jonas prompted her.

"Tiffany tripped over a bag in Jake Reeves' room and diamond earrings fell out, and when she was cleaning the newlyweds' room, she saw the couch made up as if someone had been sleeping there all night. It mightn't mean anything at all, though."

"It might mean nothing, but it might mean something," Jonas said, reaching under his hat to rub the top of his forehead. "Can Rachel and Isaac come and stay with you for a while? I'm concerned about you."

Miriam shook her head. "*Nee*, Hannah is

teething, so changing her routine might upset her. I don't want to disturb them."

"Should you speak to the bishop?" Jonas said, concern evident in his voice.

"*Nee*, I'm sure everything will be fine," Miriam said, although she was not convinced. "I just don't know whether I should tell the sheriff about the diamond earrings and the newlyweds sleeping apart." As soon as she said the words, she felt foolish. "*Nee*, of course I won't. That *does* sound rather silly, now that I think about it."

Jonas frowned. "Miriam, I'm concerned about you living here alone when the sheriff seems to think one of the guests is a jewelry thief."

Miriam waved his concerns away. "The sheriff hasn't arrested anyone, and I certainly have no jewelry to steal. If the thief is one of the guests, then surely the sheriff's visit would make a thief more cautious."

CHAPTER 5

*T*he next morning, after Miriam and Tiffany had prepared and served breakfast for all the guests, they set off for the widow Yoder's *haus*. The bishop had asked Miriam to visit Esther Yoder. She was elderly, and had insisted on living by herself for some time. The bishop had told Miriam that Esther had a daughter, but that the two of them didn't get on too well. Esther's son, a farmer, had sold his own farm in another community and bought a farm nearby. His farmhouse had a *grossmammi haus* behind it, and he was soon to move the widow Yoder into it.

Both Miriam and Tiffany had gotten up an hour earlier that morning, to attend to their chores in order to free up the time to visit the widow Yoder.

They were awfully busy at Eden with so many guests, but Miriam knew it was a priority to visit the sick, the elderly, and those in need. She also knew it would be a good experience for Tiffany to see how the Amish treated everyone.

Miriam was so lost in her own thoughts that she jumped when she realized Tiffany was speaking to her. "I'm sorry, Tiffany. What did you say?"

"I said that your new horse makes me nervous."

Miriam laughed. "He makes me a little nervous, too. He's just a typical young horse. When he gets some age and experience, he'll be just as reliable as any other horse."

Tiffany looked doubtful. "He looks like he wants to gallop away."

"He probably does," Miriam said, "but he just needs time to learn what we expect of him. He has a good temperament; he's just a little on the young side. Most young horses can be a little silly."

"So what's the story with Mrs. Yoder?" Tiffany asked her.

Miriam held onto the reins firmly as a car went past. "She's a rather independent lady, and until now has insisted on living by herself, so the bishop told me. I had the strong impression that she doesn't get on well with her daughter, but does with her son, and he's the one who's moved back here. You would have seen him at the last two meetings."

"So is Mrs. Yoder living with her son now?"

Miriam shook her head. "No, she's moving into his *grossmammi haus* soon. In fact, she should have moved there by now, but the bishop told me that she is fussing over her things and not wanting to leave her own *haus*. He wants me to encourage her to move to her son's *grossmammi haus* as soon as possible."

Tiffany gestured to the food on the back seat of the buggy. "So all that food is just our cover story?"

Miriam was confused, and said so.

Tiffany hurried to explain. "I mean, you're pretending to take her food, but your real reason is to help her realize that her son's is the best place for her to be."

Miriam laughed. "We actually *are* bringing her food, and we would take her food anyway." Miriam was amused by Tiffany's *Englischer* view of hidden agendas.

Miriam had never been to Mrs. Yoder's house before, and when she pulled the buggy to a stop outside the house, she understood the community's concerns. There was not another house in sight, and the steps to the porch were quite steep.

Tiffany helped Miriam to the door with most of the food, and Miriam knocked. "Come in," said a strong voice from inside.

They both went in, to find Mrs. Yoder sitting on a comfortable chair. "How kind of you to bring me all this food," Esther Yoder said. "Please sit with me, and I'll make you some lemon tea."

Esther stood up. "I'll help you," Miriam offered. For a moment, Miriam thought Esther would refuse her offer of help, but she readily agreed.

"I'll fetch the rest of the food from the buggy," Tiffany said, and soon disappeared from sight.

It wasn't long before the three of them were sitting in Esther's small living room, eating cookies and drinking lemon tea. Miriam was wondering how to bring the conversation around to Esther moving to her son's property, when Esther herself raised the subject.

"I'll be sorry to leave my *haus*," she said, "but I have to face facts. I'm not as young as I used to be. Last month, I fell down the steps and bruised my legs badly. I had to lie there until help came. That made me realize I can't keep living here, as much as I like my little *haus*."

Miriam nodded. "It will be sad to leave your house, but I've heard you're moving into your son's *grossmammi haus*. It sounds like you will have good times, with your son so close."

Esther looked doubtful, but added, "It will be good to have the company, I suppose. It would be even better if he finds a suitable *fraa*." She shot Miriam a calculated look, which made Miriam squirm.

Tiffany barely suppressed a giggle, and Miriam gave her a warning glance. The last thing she wanted to do was to be matched with Esther Yoder's son. Miriam knew that she was not interested in any *mann*, any *mann* but Jonas.

Miriam saw some boxes in a corner and decided to change the subject. "Have you started packing, Esther?"

Esther nodded slowly. "I have made a start, but I'm still reluctant to leave. I am in two minds about it all."

Just then, the door burst open and a tall man strode into the room. "A double minded man will receive nothing from *Der Herr*," he said firmly.

Esther waved her hand at him. "I'm not double minded, Timothy; I'm just reluctant. This is my *sonn*, Timothy Yoder. Timothy, you know Miriam Berkholder and Tiffany Bedshill?"

Timothy gave both ladies a tight-lipped smile, a

smile which did not quite reach his eyes. "*Denki* for helping my *mudder*."

"Gern gheschen," Miriam said. *You're welcome.* Tiffany simply nodded. After a few moments' awkward silence, Miriam added, "Esther was telling me she has started packing."

"*Jah*, and that's the problem," Timothy snapped. "She should have finished packing by now, not just started."

Miriam's heart went out to Esther, but Esther folded her arms over her chest. "Ferwas bischt allfatt so schtarrkeppich?" *Why are you so stubborn?* She waved one finger at him. "I'll get to that packing, all in my good time. For now, Timothy, sit down and have some of these cookies and some lemon tea. Miriam has gone to a lot of trouble to bring me all this food."

"Tiffany helped me," Miriam hurried to say.

Esther looked at her shrewdly. "And you're a widow, aren't you, Miriam?"

Miriam squirmed in her seat. "*Jah*."

Esther nodded her approval. "You must be a hard worker, running that Bed and Breakfast business all by yourself."

"All Amish are hard workers," Timothy said,

but Miriam could not help but notice that he shot her a calculating look.

The conversation was making Miriam quite uncomfortable. She hadn't expected that Timothy would be there, and his presence seemed to turn what would have been a pleasant conversation between three women into something more unsettling. There was something about Timothy that Miriam couldn't somewhat take to, but she couldn't quite figure out what it was. Maybe it was his forbidding manner.

"I have seen you at the meetings," Timothy said to Miriam, "but we have not yet had a chance to speak."

Miriam nodded. She hoped Timothy did not see her as a potential and suitable *fraa*. She wilted under Timothy's gaze. She could tell he was sizing her up, much like she imagined he would size up a prize cow for his farm. Miriam was wondering how to beat a hasty retreat. She was just about to say that she had to get back to her guests, when Esther spoke up.

"I insist you and Tiffany stay for lunch."

Miriam protested. "That's very kind of you, but we must be getting back to my guests."

"Nonsense." Esther waved a hand at her. "We'll

have an early lunch, and Timothy and you can get to know each other better."

Miriam expected Timothy would object, but to her dismay, he said he thought it was a good idea.

The lunch proved to be most uncomfortable. Not only had Miriam not had a chance to encourage Esther to move to Timothy's *grossmammi haus* sooner, but it was clear to her that Timothy had taken some sort of an interest in her. He asked her many probing questions about how long ago her husband had died, and when she had moved to Eden from Ohio, and asked about her daughter, Rachel, and how long Rachel had been married to Isaac. Miriam was a private person and did not like answering such prying questions, but to refuse or deflect would have been rude, so she had no choice but to answer them.

Finally, she was able to leave, and breathed a sigh of relief. Timothy stood on the front porch and waved to her. Miriam drove away a little faster than she should have, given that the horse was young and inexperienced.

CHAPTER 6

*W*hen the time came to have dinner that night, Miriam was in two minds. Miriam as a rule served all the guests dinner twice a week, and tonight, all the guests would be in attendance, but so would Jonas. James would be there, too, with his wife, Martha, who used to work for Miriam, and Jonas's other worker, Ethan, would also be there, a fact that would make Tiffany quite happy. The bishop had told Miriam he was pleased with Tiffany's progress, but Tiffany and Ethan were not yet allowed to date. Still, everyone knew that they soon would be able to date, and that had the two of them in a state of happiness.

If only Miriam could be as happy. The last thing she wanted to do was to be sitting for hours in what felt like a *familye* situation with Jonas, when she had no idea what she meant to him, or even if she meant anything to him at all. Still, she cherished every moment she was around him, despite the pain it caused her.

Finally, Miriam and Tiffany served everyone pork chops with sauerkraut and potatoes, and filled their glasses with spicy lemonade.

Bruce Hanson, in particular, appeared pleased with the lemonade. "What tart, sweet lemonade," he said. "It's a good old fashioned drink, with a delightfully intense lemon flavor."

His wife agreed. "Did you make it yourself?" she asked Miriam. "If so, may I have the recipe?"

Miriam frowned. "I did make it myself, and I will try to write a recipe for you, but I simply throw in a bit of this, a bit of that."

Heather seemed displeased with that statement, so Miriam turned to her food. She had only just popped a piece of potato into her mouth when Jonas turned to her. "So then, what have you been doing with yourself, Miriam?"

Miriam couldn't speak with her mouth full, so swallowed quickly before answering. "What do you mean?"

Jonas shifted in his seat. "I mean, what have you been doing lately?"

Miriam was puzzled. "Doing lately?" Why would Jonas ask such a thing? He worked there, at Eden, most days of the week doing the renovations, and what's more, she saw him every second Sunday at the gathering. If anyone were to know what she was doing, it was Jonas, so why did he ask?

At this point, Isaac entered the conversation. "Today, Miriam and Tiffany helped the widow Yoder."

Rachel nodded. "Yes, but Mrs. Yoder didn't really need their help now that her *sonn*, Timothy, has moved to town to help her. You probably don't know him too well, Jonas, because he's just arrived in the community. He seems very nice. He's a widower, about the same age as my mother."

What is Rachel doing? Miriam thought. Is she trying to help me by making Jonas jealous? Perhaps she should have a word to her *dochder*. Rachel knew how Miriam felt about Jonas as she had confided in her, but she didn't think Rachel would say anything quite so obvious.

Miriam hoped that Jonas wouldn't see through the ploy to make him jealous, but when she looked up, his face was beet red. "Timothy? Why do you mention him, Rachel?" he asked.

Rachel simply shrugged and put down her fork. "*Mamm* and Tiffany met him yesterday when they went to help his *mudder*. *Mamm* spoke highly of him." She popped a piece of potato in her mouth.

Miriam shot Rachel a warning look. She had not spoken highly of Timothy Yoder at all—she merely had polite words to say about him.

"You're not planning to visit the widow Yoder again now that her *sonn* is there to help her, are you?" While Jonas apparently addressed the question to both women, he looked directly at Miriam when he spoke.

Both Rachel and Jonas stared at Miriam, which made her even more uneasy. No one spoke, and an uncomfortable silence settled over the group.

Kevin and Susan Smith were sitting at the other end of the table, and apparently had not been following the conversation. Susan leaned forward. "How long have you two been married?"

Rachel looked up, and gestured to her husband. "Us?" she asked.

Susan shook her head. "No, Miriam and Jonas."

Miriam was beyond embarrassed. A wave of

nausea hit her, and she clutched at her stomach. "We're, we're not married," she managed to stammer, all the while avoiding Jonas's eyes.

Isaac spoke up. "Jonas is doing the renovations on Eden, and he's a widower. My mother-in-law is a widow."

While Miriam was grateful to Isaac for trying to help, she felt his statement made things even worse. Why would Susan think they were married? It made the situation too uncomfortable. To make matters worse, Jonas abruptly stood to his feet. "Thank you for the meal, Miriam and Tiffany. I must leave." With that, he stood and hurried out of the room.

Miriam was shocked, and she could see Tiffany's mouth hanging open. Isaac and Rachel exchanged glances, as did James and Martha. Was the thought of being married to her so horrible that Jonas would leave the room? What was going on with that *mann*?

Miriam had no idea how she would manage to continue with the dinner, but she had no other choice. Her heart was beating out of her chest and her palms were sweaty. It was all she could do to continue sitting at the table.

Susan Smith seemed oblivious to the stir that

her words had caused, and continued to chat away, but Miriam was relieved about that. At least it turned the attention away from her.

"And was that your little dog I heard making noises last night?" Jake asked Ava.

Ava shook her head. "No, I doubt it. Do you think there was a thief outside the building?"

Heather Hanson gasped. "Yes, how could I have forgotten? The sheriff said to keep all our valuables under lock and key. Of course, no one really takes their valuables with them when traveling, but I'm sure a jewelry thief would take money as well."

Miriam sighed. She didn't know what was worse, talking about her uncomfortable relationship —or lack of relationship—with Jonas, or talking about the jewelry thief, as that could scare visitors away from Eden. Miriam sent up a silent prayer to *Gott* to help her get through the night.

Miriam was greatly relieved when it was time to fetch the Peachy Baked Apples along with the salty pretzels and ice cream. That proved to be enough of a distraction to turn everyone's thoughts to food.

"I don't like pretzels," Susan Smith said. She held one out to Ava. "Would your little dog like it?"

Ava held up a hand. "Thank you, but no. Salt is bad for dogs."

Kevin popped five pretzels into his mouth at once. "Yum," he said when he had finished his mouthful. "The taste of the salt is amazing with the ice cream."

"Yes, salted caramel used to be my favorite ice cream," Tiffany said, a faraway look in her eyes.

Miriam wondered once more if Tiffany was regretting leaving her old life, but then she saw the tender look that passed between Tiffany and Ethan.

"There's more if anyone would like some," she said. "And there are sugar cookies to have with our coffee."

Miriam found it hard to concentrate on dinner. Why did Jonas rush out like that? He had never left halfway through a meal before. Clearly, he was embarrassed that people thought he was married to Miriam. Was it simply because he thought he might be suspected of some impropriety? Or was he really so against the idea of marriage and perhaps thought he'd been leading Miriam on? What if he turned up the following day and quit his job doing the renovations?

Miriam shook her head to try to dismiss the worrying thoughts that were coming quickly, one after another. It also seemed strange that Jonas appeared to be jealous of Timothy Yoder. What other explanation could there be for the way he acted when Rachel mentioned her visit to the widow Yoder? Miriam bit her lip. She knew that *menner* often said that women were hard to understand, but Jonas was certainly very difficult to understand. Very difficult indeed.

By the time Miriam and Tiffany were back in the kitchen making the coffee and setting the sugar cookies onto plates, Miriam was still somewhat distressed about the way that events over dinner had unfolded. She would love to ask Jonas what had happened, but she knew she couldn't. They were good friends, and could discuss everything— everything, but that.

Timothy Yoder certainly seemed to like Miriam, but Miriam didn't feel the same way about him. Sure, he was certainly attractive. Years of working on the farm had given him broad shoulders and well-muscled arms. He had a strong jaw line, but there was just something about him that Miriam hadn't taken to. Was it because of her own feelings for Jonas?

Miriam shook her head to clear it. Miriam didn't like to admit her feelings for Jonas to herself. What was the point, when they did not seem to be reciprocated? She had known Jonas almost from the time she had first set foot in Eden, but he had not asked her on a buggy ride. She was a widow, and he was a widower, so there was nothing to keep them apart. The only possible reason Miriam could think of was that Jonas was not interested in her at all. He had not shown any interest in any of the other single ladies of his age in the community, so that put her heart at rest. Or maybe he had friend-zoned her.

Miriam laughed aloud.

"What are you laughing at?" Tiffany shot her a quizzical look.

Miriam smiled in return. "I'm beginning to pick up some of your *Englischer* expressions."

Tiffany laughed, too. "Don't forget, I'm Amish now."

Miriam nodded. "You are, indeed."

"I know it's not for me to say, but did you notice that Jonas seemed upset at the mention of Timothy Yoder?"

Miriam felt her cheeks flush beet red, and muttered something incomprehensible. "Come on, Tiffany, we must return to our guests."

CHAPTER 7

Miriam had not had much sleep that past night. Lately, she had been missing her husband—not so much her husband himself, but missing having a *mann* around the place. It had been hard for her, as a single woman, to run Eden and deal with all the guests. It had been even harder since her daughter, Rachel, had left to marry Isaac. Martha had been a good worker, but then she had left to marry Jonas's worker, James. Tiffany had promise to be an able replacement, but she still didn't work as hard as an Amish person.

Miriam shook her head to clear her thoughts. Truth be told, she was missing male company. She just wanted to rest her head on a tough shoulder.

She wanted to be held by a pair of strong arms and have all her worries taken away by a capable man. She wanted more than anything for that man to be Jonas, but as her father always said, *You can lead a horse to water, but you can't make him drink.*

As much as she wanted Jonas, there was nothing she could do if he didn't feel the same way. And surely, if he did feel the same way, he would have shown some sign of it by now. The only possible sign of any feelings for her were his apparent jealousy over Timothy Yoder at the previous night's dinner. True, he had left abruptly, but there could be another logical explanation for that.

Miriam felt she was clutching at straws by hoping Jonas was jealous. Her thoughts turned to Timothy Yoder. Even if Jonas didn't feel the way she did about him, there was no way she could have feelings for Timothy. He didn't make her heart leap the way that Jonas did. In fact, she had felt that way about Jonas right from the beginning, right when she had first laid eyes on him. She didn't feel there could be any other *mann* for her but Jonas.

"Help me, *Gott*," she said under her breath.

Miriam decided to walk down to the vegetable garden to pick some parsley for lunch. The guests had all been served breakfast hours ago and were all now absent from Eden, with the exception of Ava Douglas who was taking her dog, Cuddles, for a walk down to the pond. Jonas had been conspicuous by his absence all morning. Normally, he and Miriam would have a chat, but today, he had kept well out of her way.

Miriam's spirits plummeted. *I wonder if he knows my feelings for him and he's embarrassed by them?* she asked herself, feeling quite dismayed. *Nee, surely he was jealous at the mention of Timothy Yoder.* She absently watched Ava walk back from the direction of the pond clutching a large purse. Miriam looked forward to her morning talks with Jonas. Her stomach churned. Whatever was wrong with him? She sure hoped things could return to normal soon.

Miriam looked up as a buggy drawn by a large black horse came up the road at a good pace. She shielded the sun from her eyes and looked down the road, wondering who it could be. She wasn't left in doubt very long, because the horse came to a sudden stop and Timothy Yoder jumped out of the buggy. "You didn't tell me that young Miss Tiffany's car had been used in a jewelry robbery," he said by way of greeting.

Miriam did not know how to respond. "Um, err," she stammered.

Timothy walked over to her, so close that she took a step backward. "I'm worried for your safety, Miriam," he said. "Whoever robbed the jewelry store took the keys from your house, so you could be in danger."

"Who told you all the details?" she asked him, puzzled. She deliberately had not told the widow Yoder about it because she was a private person and liked to keep matters to herself. Also, she didn't like to have the news getting out, because it could potentially scare guests away. Never mind the fact that one of the guests was likely the culprit.

"The bishop's wife visited my mother last night and told her all about it," he said. "I don't think you're safe living here, a single woman all by yourself."

For some reason, his comments rankled. "That's very kind of you, but my assistant, Tiffany, is here with me, too."

Timothy raised his eyebrows. "I don't think your young assistant would be of any help if your establishment was robbed," he said in a stern tone.

Miriam wrung her hands. His manner was making her uncomfortable, but she couldn't quite tell why. Just then, she heard a deep voice behind her.

"Is there a problem?"

She spun around to see Jonas frowning deeply.

"Um, Timothy is worried about my safety."

Jonas continued to frown. "I'm concerned about your safety, too."

Miriam was shocked that Jonas agreed with Timothy. Wasn't Jonas jealous of Timothy after all? Now she was totally confused.

Jonas was still talking. "However, the sheriff says he doesn't think you're in any danger. It wasn't as if it was an armed robbery, and the thief didn't do any damage. At least this time, the robbery doesn't seem connected with the rumored treasure at Eden."

Timothy pricked up his ears. "There is treasure at Eden?"

Miriam shrugged. "So they say. One of Captain Kidd's men built a house here, and it's said he buried his gold here as well."

Timothy smiled broadly at Miriam. "You must tell me more about it some time."

Jonas cleared his throat. "It was awfully good of you to be concerned for Miriam's welfare, Timothy. We won't hold you up any longer. I am sure you need to get back to your farm and your mother. Good day."

Timothy looked as shocked as Miriam felt. She watched him carefully to see how he would react. He simply nodded at Jonas and then at Miriam, and hopped into his buggy. He turned his horse and the horse set off at a good trot back the way he had come.

Jonas made to walk away, but then hesitated and turned back to Miriam. "Miriam, are you worried? I mean, about being at Eden alone?"

Miriam shook her head. "I feel perfectly safe, Jonas."

Jonas nodded slowly. "I've given the matter a lot of thought. It seems likely that one of the guests had something to do with the robbery, but it's not certain. Let's say that one of the guests *was* involved. In that case, I'm sure that the other guests weren't involved and you have a house full of guests. That in itself means that you should be safe at night, and the sheriff doesn't think that the robber was violent."

Miriam was about to speak, but Jonas pushed on. "That doesn't mean that the robber *isn't* violent, Miriam, so please don't go outside at night. In fact, I'd feel better if you lock your bedroom door every night."

Miriam nodded again. Jonas was about to walk

away, when he turned back to her again. He opened his mouth to speak and appeared to be on the verge of saying something, but all at once, his face flushed red. He shifted from one foot to the other and then hurried away.

Miriam had no idea of what to make of the whole exchange. Why had Jonas sent Timothy Yoder away so abruptly? Could he actually be jealous? And if he *was* jealous, then why hadn't he told Miriam of his feelings for her? She had no idea. One thing for sure, Timothy Yoder certainly seemed keen on her.

Miriam had no time to be alone with her thoughts any longer, as Susan Smith ran toward her, waving her arms furiously.

CHAPTER 8

*M*iriam's stomach sank. Whatever had happened?

"It's my engagement ring!" Susan yelled, waving her arms about. "My engagement ring's missing." With that, she burst into a flood of tears.

Miriam was at a loss. "Did you lose it?" she asked.

Susan stopped crying for a moment.

"Of course not!" she snapped. "The jewelry robber stole it!"

"Let's go into the house and call the sheriff," Miriam said, trying to inject some composure into her voice. Could this be true? Could the jewelry robber really have struck at Eden? Upon reflection, she didn't know why she was so surprised. After all, the robber had stolen Tiffany's car from Eden. Surely the robber had to be one of the guests.

Susan trailed after Miriam, sobbing loudly, so loudly in fact that Miriam wondered if Susan was faking it. She had not even heard a child cry as loudly as that, but then Miriam silently chided herself for being so unkind. While Amish didn't wear rings, Miriam knew that rings were often very important to *Englischers*, and no doubt, Susan considered her engagement ring a symbol of her love for Kevin.

When they reached the house, Kevin came down the stairs, and Susan threw herself into his arms. "It's my engagement ring!" she said in an anguished tone. "The robber stole it!"

It seemed to Miriam that Kevin didn't look overly surprised, but then again, maybe she was growing too suspicious.

"Are you sure you didn't lose it?" Kevin asked calmly.

"No," Susan said. "I was taking a bath and left it in my room. When I went back into the room, it was missing. I left it on that old chest of drawers. I looked all around the floor and everything, but there's no sign of it. What's more, the window was open and I had definitely shut it before I took a bath. It must be a cat burglar."

Miriam was puzzled. "Cat burglar?" she asked, before remembering that Ava had mentioned the term before.

Susan nodded. "Yes, you know, someone who climbs up buildings to rob things." She was speaking more calmly now. "We'll have to call the sheriff," she added. "First of all we should go and make sure nothing else is missing."

When the two of them went back to their room to see if anything else was missing, Miriam called the sheriff. She was dismayed. For some reason, the robber had turned his or her attention to Eden, and Miriam was sure the robberies would continue.

Kevin and Susan met Miriam in the foyer just as the sheriff arrived. Miriam opened the door to him. "That was fast, Sheriff."

He nodded. "Good afternoon, Mrs. Berkholder."

Before he had a chance to say more, Jonas hurried in. "Is everything all right?"

All of a sudden, Miriam felt tears prick at the corner of her eyes and she swallowed a sob. "Mrs. Smith's engagement ring is missing."

"It went missing from our room," Susan added.

"Why don't you show me where you left it," the sheriff said, "and then we can all sit down and talk about this."

The sheriff followed Kevin and Susan Smith up the stairs, while Miriam turned to Jonas. "Oh Jonas, I'm so worried. I'm sure these robberies won't stop now that they've started in the *haus*."

Jonas stroked his chin. "I don't like it, Miriam. I don't like it at all."

"What am I going to do, Jonas?" Miriam asked, dismayed to hear her voice come out as a wail.

"I'll think of something, Miriam," Jonas said. "Please don't worry yourself about it." He seemed about to say more, when Tiffany hurried down the stairs.

"I heard what the sheriff said," she said. "Susan Smith's engagement ring has gone missing."

Miriam nodded. "Yes, that's right."

"Insurance fraud!" Tiffany pronounced dramatically.

Miriam had no idea what she was talking about. "What do you mean, Tiffany?"

Tiffany frowned. "Kevin and Susan Smith told the sheriff that they had to contact their insurance company at once and make a claim. Did you see Susan's engagement ring?"

Miriam shrugged. All engagement rings looked the same to her. Rings meant nothing to Amish, considering they never wore jewelry.

Unperturbed by Miriam's less than enthusiastic reaction, Tiffany pushed on. "It was very small and plain, probably just an industrial diamond chip. I heard them tell the sheriff it was worth ten thousand dollars."

"Ten thousand dollars?" Miriam said in shock. She exchanged glances with Jonas.

Tiffany was still talking. "There's no way her engagement ring was worth ten thousand dollars, which makes me think it's insurance fraud."

Jonas crossed his arms over his chest. "Do you mean they hid their engagement ring, and lied about it being stolen to claim money from their insurance company under false pretenses?"

Tiffany nodded. "Yes, that's exactly what I'm saying."

At that point, the sheriff came downstairs and Miriam led him into the living room. She and Jonas sat on the heavy couch opposite the sheriff, while Tiffany scurried away to attend to her duties.

Miriam wasted no time telling the sheriff of Tiffany's suspicions.

The sheriff nodded slowly. "To tell you the

truth, that occurred to me, too. Still, I don't want to jump to any conclusions. I'll look into their background. Meanwhile, Mrs. Berkholder, do you think it's wise to keep Eden open while all this is happening?"

Miriam was aghast. "You don't mean I should turn the guests away and tell them to stay somewhere else?"

The sheriff avoided her gaze. "Yes, that's exactly what I'm saying. At least until this business is over."

"But I can't," Miriam protested. "I've worked so hard to get Eden up and running, and now I have all these guests that I worked so hard to get! I can't turn them away just because someone used Tiffany's car to rob a jewelry store in town, and because the Smiths say that their engagement ring is missing. Why, for all we know, it could have fallen down a crack in the floor boards." She shot Jonas a look, but he was clearly uncomfortable. She figured he was torn between wanting to support her, and at the same time worried for her safety.

"Do you really think someone climbed up into the Smiths' room from outside just to steal the ring?" she asked the sheriff.

The sheriff shook his head. "Unless someone

had a mighty tall ladder, I can't see how that was possible. I'm not saying I disbelieve them, but I'm not saying I believe them, either. I need to check out their background. Meanwhile, Mrs. Berkholder, could you ask your daughter and son-in-law to stay with you for a while?"

Miriam wrung her hands. "No, their baby's teething and I don't want to disrupt her routine. If anything else happens, though, I will," she added for Jonas's benefit. "Sheriff, are you any closer to finding out who robbed the store?"

The sheriff shook his head. "I wish I had better news for you, but as it stands, we haven't got very far with our investigations. It also seems strange that no other jewelry stores have been robbed. Usually, we don't get isolated incidents like this. This is very puzzling."

Miriam rubbed her forehead to ease away the headache that was threatening to form. "Very puzzling indeed," she said sadly.

CHAPTER 9

*J*ust then, there was a loud knock on the door. The sheriff stood up and tipped his hat. "If you'll excuse me, I had better get back to work."

Miriam opened the door for him, and for Jonas who followed the sheriff out, and then all but gasped in shock when she saw Debra Bedshill on her porch.

Debra was wearing a tight cream suit, with a brightly patterned red and cream floral scarf wrapped around her neck, and her heels were so high that Miriam wondered how she could possibly walk in them. If Debra had been a horse, she would be well and truly lame by now.

When Miriam had first inherited Eden and had

moved there with her daughter, Rachel, the Bedshills had been a thorn in her side. Debra and her husband ran a Bed and Breakfast establishment in town, and they did everything they could to make Miriam's life difficult. They ordered tradesmen not to help Miriam, and even once drove to Eden to tell Miriam she should go back to Ohio. However, that all changed when Debra appeared at Eden one day and asked Miriam to take on Tiffany as an assistant. She had said the girl was spoiled, and wanted her to learn some good old-fashioned discipline.

Tiffany had not only learned some old-fashioned discipline, but had fallen in love with Ethan, the Amish man who worked for Jonas, and what's more, had even joined the community. Tiffany had come back very upset from the meeting with her parents when she told them she was joining the Amish community, and Tiffany had not spoken to them since. Miriam likewise had not spoken to the Bedshills since. She had been on the receiving end of a tongue lashing from Debra once before, and did not really fancy another one.

With that in mind, Miriam quickly searched Debra's face to see if she could gauge her mood. "May I come in?" Debra said sternly.

Miriam stood aside. "Of course." She showed

Debra into the living room and indicated that she should sit. "Would you like some meadow tea, or perhaps a glass of lemonade?"

"No, thank you," Debra said through pursed lips.

At that moment, Bruce and Heather Hanson returned from their outing. They stopped dead in their tracks when they saw Debra Bedshill.

"Mr. and Mrs. Hanson!" Debra said with obvious surprise. "What are you doing here? I thought you had finished your vacation."

Bruce and Heather exchanged glances and both their faces flushed beet red. It was obvious to Miriam that they were guilty, but about what? Had they disliked Debra's establishment so much that they had gone straight to Eden? That couldn't be right. As abrupt as Debra was, her Bed and Breakfast had a fine reputation.

"We were going straight home when we saw an ad for Eden, and wanted to try the Amish experience while we were still in Pennsylvania," Bruce said.

At his words, his wife nodded vigorously. "That's right; that's right," she said, still nodding her head.

Miriam was certain they were lying. She didn't

like to have such unkind thoughts, but it was clear that they were covering something up. Debra seemed to be of the same opinion. Debra narrowed her eyes and continued to stare at the couple more closely.

Bruce grabbed his wife's hand. "Well, if you'll excuse us. It was nice to see you again, Mrs. Bedshill." With that, the couple hurried out of the room as fast as they possibly could.

Debra looked after them for a while, and then turned back to Miriam. "Is my daughter here?"

Miriam nodded. "Would you like me to fetch her?"

Debra shook her head. "I have come to speak to you, and what I have to say is for your ears only."

Miriam's stomach churned, and she tried to school her face into an impassive expression.

"I'm going to order Tiffany to return to us, and I don't want you to stand in her way," Debra said firmly. "The sheriff has informed us that Tiffany's car was used in a jewelry robbery recently."

"Tiffany had nothing to do with that," Miriam hurried to say. "The keys were here, in a kitchen drawer, and someone stole them. Surely you don't think it was Tiffany?"

Debra waved a hand in dismissal. "To be quite

frank, I don't know what to think. Tiffany obviously has issues, and there is no telling what she'll do next. She is obviously very unreliable and even more impulsive. She acts before she thinks things through. Tiffany needs to come home, right now!"

Miriam let out a long breath slowly. "It is entirely up to Tiffany as to what she decides to do," she said. "It's entirely her decision."

Debra gestured up and down Miriam. "Surely you can see it's not normal for her to want to be like you!"

Miriam didn't quite know how to take her words. "It is unusual for an *Englischer* to join the community," she began slowly, but Debra interrupted her.

"It's nonsense!" she snapped. "It's utter nonsense. It's just ridiculous, if you ask me. The girl has gone from one extreme to another. First of all she was a spoiled little brat, and now she's gone the opposite and has become a goody goody two shoes. Why couldn't she have found a middle road? She always *was* a difficult child."

Miriam shifted in her seat, completely at a loss. It was a great relief that Jonas came back into the room. He marched straight over to Mrs. Bedshill. "How may I be of assistance?"

Debra, for once, seemed to be at a loss. "I was just telling Mrs. Berkholder here that I'm going to order Tiffany to come back home, and I've asked her not to interfere in any way."

"No one has any desire to stop Tiffany from making her own decisions," he said, but Miriam noticed that his comment only seem to rankle Debra.

"Why is she staying here with you, then?" Debra addressed the question directly to Miriam.

Jonas answered for her. "You'd have to ask Tiffany that yourself. Shall I fetch her for you?" He left the room before Debra could speak, leaving a weighty, uncomfortable silence hanging in the air, a silence so heavy that Miriam almost felt she could reach out and touch it.

Tiffany looked even more alarmed to see Debra than Miriam had been. "Hello, Mom," she said nervously.

Jonas took Miriam by the arm. "We'll give you two some time alone," he said as he and Miriam hurried from the room.

"Let's walk down to the pond," Miriam said. "That should be far enough away."

Jonas laughed. Miriam was pleased to see him laugh—she hadn't seen him laugh for a while. At that moment, whatever had been troubling him seem to have been washed away. "Thanks for coming to my rescue, Jonas," she added.

Jonas slowed his stride for a moment. "I'll always come to your rescue, Miriam," he said.

Miriam's heart fluttered at his words, and at his proximity to her. Whatever did he mean by that? Were they the words a friend would say to another friend? She wasn't sure. To cover her embarrassment, Miriam broke into fast speech. "You don't think Tiffany will go back with her *mudder*, do you? Do you think Debra will yell at her? I feel so sorry for Tiffany."

"*Gott* will have his way," Jonas said calmly. "*Gott* cares for the birds of the air and for all of us. Look at those little ducklings, Miriam."

Miriam stopped and took a deep breath. It certainly was a tranquil scene in front of her. Five little ducklings floated behind their mother on the pond and a gentle breeze blew against the wisp of hair that had escaped from her bonnet. Just then, a barking dog disturbed the peace.

"I'm so sorry," Ava Douglas's voice called out. "Cuddles is being very naughty today." She appeared round the corner, clutching her hip and limping. "I wish I'd had the hip replacement before

I had taken this vacation. I'm certainly regretting that decision now."

Miriam at once went to her. "Are you in much pain, Mrs. Douglas?" she asked with concern.

Ava waved her concerns away. "I'm fine, I'm fine. There's no need to fuss. I'll be right as rain once I get that nice new hip. I only hope I don't need both my knees replaced. The doctor said it was a strong possibility." Soon her frown was replaced by a smile. "Never mind, today is a lovely day and running after Cuddles keeps me young."

"Would you like some help back to the house?" Miriam asked her.

Ava shook her head. "I wish I was as agile as Kevin Smith."

Miriam and Jonas looked at each other. "What do you mean?" Jonas asked her.

Ava pointed to where the little track around the pond ran into some thick trees. "He was hurrying in there with a backpack. Perhaps he's training for a marathon or something. Who goes running with a backpack? I thought it was very strange, and he certainly didn't want to be seen. Oh well, it's none of my business."

Ava limped off with her little dog, leaving Miriam worriedly looking after her.

"What you make of that, Jonas?" she asked him.

Jonas shook his head. "The sheriff said he'd look into the Smiths. It does seem a bit suspicious that Kevin Smith was acting furtively and went somewhere where he wouldn't be seen with a backpack." He shot a look at Miriam. "Don't worry about it, Miriam. If he has a criminal record, the sheriff will turn it up in no time at all."

Miriam wrung her hands nervously. "But Jonas, surely the sheriff should have checked if any of the guests had a criminal background by now? And he hasn't discovered anything. Jonas, I don't know what to do."

Jonas took a step toward her. "Miriam…"

CHAPTER 10

*M*iriam looked up at Jonas. She hadn't seen him wearing that expression before. He was serious, but there was some other deep emotion. Fear? Trepidation? She could not be sure.

"Miriam," Jonas said again, "we've known each other a long time now. Well, ever since you came to Eden. I don't suppose that was a very long time ago, but it really *was* a long time ago when you think about it. After all, your *dochder* Rachel married Isaac, and now they have a *boppli*, but when you came to Eden, Rachel and Isaac hadn't even met, so I suppose you *could* call it a long time ago." He hesitated and scratched his chin. "Although, I suppose, some people wouldn't call it a long time ago. I do," he added, avoiding her eyes.

Miriam was suddenly confused. Was he going to quit working for her as her builder? "You haven't finished the renovation work yet," she said in a small voice.

Her words seemed to surprise Jonas. He frowned deeply and then shifted from one foot to another. "No, I haven't." He continued to look confused. They stood there in silence for a long moment, before Jonas pushed on. "Miriam, it's been a long time since my *fraa* died, and I know it's been a long time since your husband died. Of course, some might not call it a long time, but I call it a long time. I was wondering if you call it a long time, too?"

Miriam was more confused than ever. "*Jah,*" she said, wondering where on earth this conversation was going. "Jonas, are you saying you don't want to continue to do the renovation work at Eden?"

A spark of realization flashed across Jonas's face. "*Nee*! *Nee,* I wasn't talking about that at all. Sorry, have I been confusing?"

Miriam nodded, but before she could speak, a tall figure appeared around the cover of the hickory trees. It was Timothy Yoder.

He waved as he strode over to the pair. Ignoring Jonas, he stood squarely in front of Miriam. "I heard about the jewelry robbery at Eden."

Miriam gasped. "But it only just happened!"

Timothy shrugged. "The sheriff came over to tell my mother to be careful, given that she lives nearby, and I happened to be there. He told me about the robbery at Eden."

"The sheriff isn't even sure it *is* a robbery yet," Jonas interjected. "It was only one piece of jewelry, an engagement ring, and it may even have been lost."

Timothy pursed his lips and looked at Miriam once more. Ignoring Jonas's words, he said to Miriam, "Mer muss uff sich selwer achtgewwe." *You have to take care of yourself.*

Miriam was beginning to get a little tired of Timothy's attention. She had given him not the slightest bit of encouragement, yet he was acting quite proprietarily toward her. What's more, he had interrupted whatever Jonas had wanted to say to her. She had no idea what that was, but it had obviously been awfully important to Jonas, so Timothy's timing could not have been worse.

Before Miriam could respond to Timothy, she heard yelling over by the hickory trees. The three of them spun around to see Susan yelling at Kevin, waving her arms at him. Susan seemed quite angry, and Kevin took a step backward. Susan snatched his backpack from him, looked inside it, took something out, and then threw both the object and the backpack to the ground.

Jonas and Miriam exchanged glances. "I wonder what all that's about?" Miriam said. "Susan seems very upset."

She continued to watch the scene unfold, but then Kevin picked up his backpack and trailed after Susan who stormed off in Miriam's direction. *They're coming this way*, Miriam thought. *It will get a little awkward if they realize that we observed the whole scene.*

Susan was the first one to round the corner and come upon the trio. She gasped, and her hand flew to her mouth. Nevertheless, she recovered her composure quickly. "Hello, everyone."

Miriam introduced Timothy Yoder, who simply pursed his lips and nodded. Kevin caught up to Susan, and Miriam likewise introduced him to Timothy. Susan then reached back for Kevin's hand, and gave him a big kiss on the cheek. The two of them walked away, their arms around one another.

Miriam thought back to when Tiffany had said that someone had slept on the couch in their bedroom. Clearly, Kevin and Susan were covering something up. Was it simply an attempt to cover up marital discord, considering they were newlyweds? Miriam shook her head. It was none of her business, unless of course, they were the jewelry thieves.

She looked up to see Timothy staring at her, which made her uncomfortable. "I'd like to speak to you in private, Miriam," Timothy said, shooting a look from under his bushy eyebrows at Jonas. His words came out more as a strong demand than a request.

Jonas appeared decidedly unhappy. Miriam likewise was not happy, but she did not know how to refuse Timothy. To do so would be rude.

"We'll continue our previous conversation later," Jonas said to Miriam. He looked none too pleased.

Timothy waited until Jonas was well out of earshot before turning back to Miriam. "Miriam, I'm worried about you being by yourself with a criminal on the loose."

Miriam had no idea how to respond, so simply nodded.

"Miriam, I've given it a lot of thought, and I've come to the conclusion we should get married."

Miriam gasped. She had certainly not expected to hear those words out of Timothy's mouth. In her imagined worst case scenario, she had figured he might ask her to go on a buggy ride—but marriage? "Married?" Miriam echoed.

Timothy nodded solemnly. "It's not good for a woman your age to be living alone and running a business. I suggest a companion marriage."

"A companion marriage?' Miriam repeated. "What is that?"

Timothy frowned. "It's just a normal marriage. I suppose you haven't heard that term before as you're from another community. I don't like children, so I want a companion marriage, that is, one where we won't have *kinner*. A family formation marriage would be one where I married a younger woman, one of child-bearing age, and had a *familye*. I've never been married, but I don't mind taking on a widow of your age. You will come and live with me on my farm, and sell Eden."

"Sell Eden?" Miriam repeated. She was a little annoyed with herself for simply echoing Timothy's words, but she was in a considerable amount of shock. She was also offended by his words. "I have no intention of selling Eden," Miriam said, saying the first thing that was on her mind. "My *grossmammi* left it to me, and I've put a lot of work into it. What's more, I enjoy running the business." Miriam once more silently chastised herself for her words. Why was she defending herself? She had no intention whatsoever of marrying Timothy Yoder, or even going with him on a buggy ride for that matter.

Timothy pursed his lips tightly, so much so, that they formed a thin line. He frowned down on her with a look of stern disapproval. "Perhaps we could rent out Eden rather than sell it, if you really insist," he added, "but I would prefer to sell it. Anyway, that could be a matter for further discussion. I need help around my farm, so you can come and live with me once we're married."

Miriam could feel her anger rising within her, and sent up a silent apology to *Gott* for her temper. It was all she could do not to stomp her foot. "Thank you for your kind offer, Timothy," she said through clenched teeth, "but I shall not be marrying you. I have no feelings toward you, and so I won't be marrying you."

"Feelings, *pshaat*!" Timothy said with disdain. "What do feelings have to do with marriage? This is a suitable marriage, by all accounts. You won't have to work anymore running a business as that is most unseemly for a single woman your age, and you can live on my farm and assist me instead. That is a far more suitable arrangement. I'm sure we will grow to be fond of each other in time."

"I said no, Timothy. Please accept my decision. There will be no further discussion of this matter." With that, Miriam turned on her heel and hurried away. She listened for footsteps, but thankfully there were none. She was afraid Timothy would come after her to insist.

As Miriam approached Eden, she saw that Debra Bedshill's car was still there. This had certainly been a most difficult day. As Miriam approached the porch, Debra walked out. When she saw Miriam, she stopped and waited for her.

Miriam's heart caught in her mouth. She hoped this was not going to be yet another difficult conversation. "Did you speak to Tiffany?" she asked Debra, and then clutched her stomach, waiting for a verbal tirade.

To her surprise, Debra's expression was more mellow than earlier. "Yes," she said simply. "We had quite a good talk. To my surprise, Tiffany seems more mature than she's ever been before, and she even talked sense and didn't yell at me. Maybe this…"— Debra broke off and appeared to be searching for the right word—"lifestyle," she continued, "is doing the girl some good, much to my surprise." Debra nodded curtly and made to march past Miriam.

Miriam remembered something and called after her. "Do you mind if I ask you a question about the Hansons?"

Debra spun on her heel, a look of shock on her face. "What is it?"

"You said they booked at your establishment and then said they had finished their vacation and were returning home. You seemed surprised to see them here." Miriam knew it was a statement and not a question, but she did not like to ask Debra outright if the pair had been acting suspiciously, or whether Debra thought they could be the jewelry thieves.

Debra appeared to be thinking it over for a moment. "Yes, they said that, and I *was* surprised to see them here. I had to keep a close eye on those two. I found they behaved strangely on several occasions, so I was keeping a very close eye on them."

So Miriam had been right after all. "What did they do?" she asked with interest.

"On one occasion, I caught Bruce Hanson in my office, looking at my laptop," she said. "I asked him what he was doing, and he said he was looking for the internet password. I knew that wasn't true, so I wondered if he was working for the IRS. Still, I'm sure the IRS doesn't sneak around doing things like that, so I had no idea what he was up to. I didn't know what, but I was sure he was up to something. I also saw Heather slipping one of my menus into her purse, and they took copious amounts of photographs. Now, I must be off."

As Debra hurried back to her car, Miriam gave the matter some thought. Bruce and Heather Hanson had also taken abundant photographs of Eden. She had thought they were fascinated by the Amish way of life, but then again it seemed they had done that at Debra's place as well. What on earth could they be up to? And if they were the jewelry thieves, why would they steal a menu and take photographs? It certainly didn't make sense.

Miriam looked around the house for Jonas. He was nowhere to be seen, but she really wanted to tell him of her conversation with Timothy. It had upset her considerably and she needed a strong shoulder to lean on.

Miriam headed straight for the kitchen to make herself a nice cup of meadow tea, but to her surprise, Kevin was there, bending over, looking in a cupboard. He swung around when he saw her. "I'm so sorry!" he said. "I know guests aren't allowed in here. It's just that I'm really, really hungry." At that point, his stomach rumbled loudly, seemingly in agreement with his words. Kevin's face turned a pale shade of pink.

Miriam thought his behavior suspicious, but gestured to the kitchen table. "Please sit down, and I'll fetch you something to eat."

Kevin beamed at her and took a seat at the table. "Please don't go to any trouble on my account. I'm just after something very quick to eat. My wife has me on a strict diet." He laughed ruefully and patted his stomach.

"Would you like some bread soup?" Miriam asked him.

Kevin looked puzzled. "What is it?"

"I'll take some of that bread I made two days ago and tear it into some pieces and put them in a soup bowl. Then I'll put some fresh fruit on it and pour milk over the top."

Kevin's face lit up. Miriam set about preparing the bread soup, all the while wondering what Bruce and Heather Hanson were up to, what was in Kevin's backpack that Susan had thrown to the ground—could it have been stolen jewelry and Susan had found out that her husband was the thief?—and why had Timothy proposed to her out of the blue when they had not even dated, and where on earth was Jonas?

CHAPTER 11

*M*iriam had to attend a viewing that afternoon. Mr. Lapp, an elderly *mann* from the community, had gone to be with *Gott* earlier in the week. The viewing was that afternoon, and the funeral was the following day.

Although Miriam really needed Tiffany to stay and attend to the guests, she felt that going to a viewing and a funeral would be good for Tiffany to help her become more accustomed to the Amish ways.

Tiffany helped her pack the funeral pies into the buggy. "Why are they called funeral pies again?" Tiffany asked her.

Miriam sighed. She hoped Tiffany would not ask too many questions that she had already answered previously. "I explained this yesterday when we were making the pies," Miriam said patiently.

Tiffany looked somewhat embarrassed. "I forgot. I remember why they have raisins, though. Oh sorry, I've forgotten again."

Miriam sighed again. She expected Tiffany's mind was elsewhere, namely on Ethan. She took a deep breath and set about explaining funeral pies once more. "Funeral pies are the traditional gift to give the *familye* of someone who has passed away."

"Why is that?" Tiffany asked, this time paying attention.

"Funeral pies keep well and can be made a day or more before the funeral," Miriam explained. "Before people had gas refrigerators, they didn't always have fresh fruit, but they usually had dried fruit. The ingredients are found in most homes: raisins, of course, and cornstarch, cinnamon or various spices, vinegar, butter, and the ingredients for the dough. The pies keep without refrigeration."

"But you put milk in the ones we made," Tiffany asked, puzzled.

"You don't need milk to make a funeral pie," Miriam explained. "Ours do have milk and so will have a custard pie taste to them. Of course, I have a refrigerator, which is why I put milk in the pies."

Tiffany nodded. "That makes sense. Do funeral pies all look like the ones we made, double-crusted pies with lattice tops?"

"Usually," Miriam said, "but there are some variations. Now let's fetch the potato salad. Remember, some of this food will be used tomorrow, but the women are bringing most of it today."

Tiffany fetched the first of the potato salad from the refrigerator. "It's all very well organized, isn't it?"

Miriam laughed. "Yes, very well organized. Now, do you remember what happens at a viewing?"

Tiffany bit her lip and looked off into the distance. "The coffins are simple and made of pine. They have six sides, and there are two pieces on hinges that fold down to show the body from the chest up. The body will be dressed in white clothing."

Miriam was impressed. "You remembered all that very well indeed."

"I also know that the viewings can last for three

days after someone dies, and that I have to sit quietly in a room at the person's *haus*."

Miriam nodded. "*Jah*, you remembered correctly. One of the *familye* will ask us if we want to see the body, and we will go to the coffin briefly."

When Miriam arrived at the Lapps' *haus*, she saw Rachel and Isaac arrive with their *boppli*, Hannah. Miriam hurried over to them. "We won't stay long, what with Hannah teething," Rachel said.

"We can't stay long, either," Miriam said. Isaac loaded himself up with food and headed into the Lapps' house, with Tiffany trailing behind him, while Rachel caught Miriam's arm.

"How are things with Jonas?" she whispered.

Miriam looked around nervously. "Shush, Rachel. Someone might hear you."

Rachel laughed, balancing the baby on her hip. "You haven't answered my question."

"Nothing is happening with Jonas. What do you mean, Rachel?"

Rachel shot her mother a look. "You can't deny you're in love with Jonas, *Mamm*. You've already told me that."

Miriam did not know how to respond. After a few more steps, she whispered, "Yes, I am, but he doesn't feel the same way."

Rachel looked surprised. "Of course he does!"

Miriam stopped and turned to face Rachel. "How long have we been at Eden?" Without waiting for her *dochder* to answer, she spoke again. "And all that time, Jonas has never shown any interest in me."

"Yes, he has…" Rachel began, but Miriam interrupted her.

"Jonas has been getting uncomfortable lately when the two of us have been talking."

"That's because he has feelings for you," Rachel protested, "and I'm sure he has no idea of your feelings for him. I know he charges you a very low rate for all the renovation work, and I'm sure that's so he can stay around Eden, just so he can see you."

They had reached the house, so Miriam could say no more. She sat down on one of the benches that the community had placed in two of the rooms for the viewing. She looked around for Jonas, but couldn't see him. She had no idea if he was attending the viewing that afternoon, because he hadn't told her. That was unlike him.

Soon it was Miriam's and Tiffany's turn to view the body. The white cloth was pulled back to reveal Mr. Lapp's face. Tiffany gripped Miriam's arm, and Miriam patted her hand reassuringly.

After some time, Miriam sought out Mrs. Lapp. "*Gott* saw fit to take my husband," Mrs. Lapp said by way of greeting. "Did you know he was my second husband?"

Miriam said that she did not know.

Mrs. Lapp nodded. "My first husband died after we had five children, and then I had another three children with my new husband. I was blessed." She gasped and turned around.

Miriam turned around, too, and saw that a black-capped chickadee was sitting on the coffin. "I'll try to coax it outside," she said to Mrs. Lapp, relieved to see a brief smile flitter across Mrs. Lapp's face.

The cheeky bird took a considerable deal of coaxing and flew around the room several times before leaving through the open door, much to the delight of the *kinner* present. *If only Jonas had been here to help*, Miriam thought, but then that was a regular sentiment for her. She always wished Jonas was there, no matter what she was doing.

On the way home in the buggy, Tiffany chatted away about the viewing, but Miriam's thoughts drifted away to what Mrs. Lapp had said. Mrs. Lapp had found happiness after being widowed.

Yet would Miriam ever know such happiness?

Would she ever find love again? She had feelings for Jonas, deep feelings—that much she could admit to herself, but did he feel the same way about her? It didn't seem so, no matter how much Miriam wished it to be true. They had been at Eden long enough for Rachel to find a husband and even have a *boppli*, yet Jonas had not shown interest in Miriam. Jonas had been a widower for some years, so perhaps he intended never to marry again.

Miriam's heart sank at the thought.

CHAPTER 12

The following day was the funeral itself, and Miriam had not spoken to Jonas since the previous day. Miriam and Tiffany were sitting on the bench seats. Tiffany leaned across and whispered to Miriam, "Please don't think I'm being rude, Miriam, but I think I've adapted fairly well to the Amish way of life." Before Miriam could speak, Tiffany held up a hand. "I'm not being boastful or anything, but I said that simply to say that I'm having a lot of trouble getting used to the church meetings." Her hand flew to her mouth. "Sorry, I know you don't call them *church* meetings, just *meetings*. But it's just that they seem to go on for ever and ever!"

Miriam smiled to herself at Tiffany's sad tone.

"You're saying that you find the talks boring?" Tiffany turned beet red, so Miriam added, "Listen to what the ministers have to say, because their words are wise. If you get distracted, you will be bored, but try to listen to what they say and pay attention."

Tiffany nodded, but Miriam did not think she looked convinced. Miriam had been born and raised Amish, and she understood that someone born and raised an *Englischer* could easily be bored by the meetings that went for hours.

Miriam tapped Tiffany's knee. "Hush now. The helpers have just arrived, so it's about to begin."

The first minister spoke for an hour, as did the next minister. Both spoke words of praise to *Gott*, but Miriam realized she had not followed her own advice to Tiffany. She had not listened to the words of wisdom from the ministers, because her thoughts were firmly with Jonas. By the time the bishop read a hymn and then mentioned Mr. Lapp's name, his birth date and death date, Miriam was still wondering about Jonas's feelings for her.

When she and Tiffany were finally in the buggy, and in a procession of buggies following the buggy that served as the hearse, Miriam turned to Tiffany. "What did you think of the service?"

Tiffany shrugged. "I did my best to listen to the wise words, but one thing surprised me."

"What was that?"

"The bishop and the ministers didn't say anything at all about Mr. Lapp. At an *Englischer* funeral, all they ever talk about is the person who died."

Miriam nodded. "I've heard that before."

"Why didn't they mention Mr. Lapp?" Tiffany persisted.

Miriam wasn't quite sure how to answer that. "I suppose because he's no longer here," she said tentatively. "It's not the Amish way to mention the deceased at a funeral."

"That's weird," Tiffany said, quickly followed by, "No offense. How long will the service last at the cemetery?"

Miriam could not help but smile at Tiffany's tone. "It's very fast," she said. "The minister will read a hymn, and then the coffin will be lowered into the grave."

Tiffany's face brightened up. "Is that all? What else happens?"

Miriam shook her head. "Nothing. Nothing else happens. Then most people will go to the Lapps' house for food, but we have to go back to Eden. We have a mountain of laundry to do."

"Laundry," Tiffany said gleefully.

Miriam hid a smile. Obviously, Tiffany would rather do laundry than listen to another long talk by one of the ministers. Miriam realized she had not yet asked Tiffany how she was faring after her conversation with her mother. Still, Tiffany's demeanor seemed cheerful enough.

Miriam raised her eyebrows. "I'm glad to see you're okay, after your talk with your *mudder*."

Tiffany nodded. "I was quite scared to see her at first, but she seemed to calm down and she was almost reasonable." Tiffany gave a dry laugh. "It started off badly, but it got better and better as time went on. I don't even think she was all that angry with me in the end."

Miriam smiled with relief. "That is *gut* news. That was the impression I had, too."

When Miriam reached the cemetery, Tiffany exclaimed aloud. "The headstones are all the same! They're little, and white." She looked around for a few more moments before speaking again. "The headstones don't have angels or crosses on them. I know; don't tell me. It's the Amish way."

Miriam nodded, but she had spotted Jonas's

buggy. He caught her eye and nodded to her, but then walked in the opposite direction.

Miriam's heart fell, but one thing she was grateful for—Timothy Yoder had not spoken to her again. That probably had something to do with the fact that she was doing her best to avoid him, but she knew he wasn't one to take no for an answer. She figured he would propose again sooner or later, and she certainly wasn't looking forward to that.

CHAPTER 13

*J*onas had been conspicuous by his absence for the remainder of the day, although Miriam had seen him from a distance. She even began to wonder if he would come for dinner that night, as was his habit.

That night, Miriam had invited all the guests for dinner. Miriam usually provided dinner for the guests twice a week, but had decided to busy herself by preparing yet another dinner for them. It wasn't as if she didn't have enough work to do, but thoughts of Jonas made her stomach churn and her heart race, and the harder she worked, the more those thoughts kept away, so work harder she did.

Tonight, Miriam intended to serve meatloaf

with creamed celery and a variety of vegetables, and for dessert, caramel pudding, banana pudding, and shoo fly pie.

At that point, Tiffany entered the kitchen. Tiffany's time since the funeral had been filled with laundry and general cleaning. "One thing I like about the Amish is that there is always more than one dessert," Tiffany said by way of greeting. "When I was an *Englischer*, we only ever had one dessert, but Amish can have up to five desserts at the one meal."

The sound of someone clearing his throat caused Miriam to spin around. Jonas was standing in the doorway looking awkward. Tiffany took that as her cue to leave the room, leaving Miriam and Jonas alone.

"You had a conversation with Timothy Yoder the other day," Jonas said.

Miriam nodded. She knew that Jonas would not come out and ask her what was said, but he clearly was keen to know. "Yes, Timothy asked me to marry him."

Miriam was almost amused by the expression on Jonas's face. His eyebrows shot up so rapidly and so far, that Miriam wouldn't have been surprised if they flew off his face.

"He, he did?" Jonas sputtered. His face went beet red.

Miriam nodded. "*Jah.*"

"And what did you say?" Jonas asked in a surprised voice.

"Well, I told him no, of course," Miriam said. Did Jonas really think she would accept Timothy Yoder's proposal? He certainly didn't know her as well as she thought he did.

To her surprise, Jonas's face was covered with immense relief. "You did?" he squeaked.

"Of course I turned him down, Jonas," Miriam said in a scolding tone. "I thought you of all people would know me better than that. Why on earth would I accept a proposal by Timothy Yoder?" She stopped speaking when she realized she was waving a wooden spoon at him.

For some reason, Jonas looked awfully pleased and hurried out of the room. Tiffany came straight back in. "If you don't mind me saying so, I overheard everything," Tiffany admitted. "Did Mr. Yoder really propose to you?"

Miriam nodded. "*Jah,* he did."

Tiffany looked surprised. "But the two of you hardly know each other. He didn't ask you on a buggy ride or anything?"

Miriam laughed at the look on Tiffany's face. "*Nee*. He actually asked me outright to marry him. Mind you, he wasn't proposing a marriage of love, rather a marriage of convenience."

Tiffany seemed to be digesting her words. "Is that normal? I mean, is it normal in the community to have a marriage that isn't based on love?"

Miriam shrugged. "Not in my experience, but I suppose everyone has their own ways. I'm sure it works for some people." *But it wouldn't work for me,* she added silently.

When the mashed potatoes were ready, Miriam took them out to the table. Soon all the guests were there, including Jonas, much to Miriam's relief. So too, was Jake, the author. Miriam had forgotten all about him. She wondered if he had kept under the radar because he was in fact the thief.

However, she soon abandoned that opinion, because Jake did not stop talking. "Do you realize that someone sitting at this table is a jewelry thief?" he announced loudly.

"Now, young man, it's not wise to accuse people like that," Jonas said, although not unkindly. Miriam shot him a grateful smile.

Jake did not appear to mind Jonas's words. "I'm

not accusing anyone in particular; I'm just saying it has to be someone here. It could be any one of us. I mean, I know it's not me so I know it has to be someone else. Someone stole the keys to Miss Tiffany's car, and that could have been anyone, but then someone stole Susan Smith's engagement ring."

"That's right," Susan piped up.

Jake waggled his finger at her. "Then again, and this is only hypothetical, mind you, you might be the jewelry thief and pretending someone stole your engagement ring to cover up the fact."

Susan looked horrified, and Ava giggled. Miriam noticed that Kevin took the opportunity of his wife's distraction to pile mashed potatoes onto his plate.

Jake held up his hands. "I'm not saying it's you, Susan," he hastened to add, "not at all. I'm just saying that all of us here are suspects."

Bruce Hanson looked at him through narrowed eyes. "You're not a detective, are you? I thought you were an author."

Jake nodded. "Sure, I'm an author, but all writing is autobiographical to some degree. I write about my experiences. I write murder mysteries, and I always kill people that I don't like. For example, a friend cheated me out of money, so I killed him."

Tiffany gasped. Jake laughed, and added, "In a book, I mean, Miss Tiffany. I've killed lots of people in books, but of course I've never killed anyone in person. However, if I do say so myself, I'm a good judge of human nature and I know when people are more than they pretend to be."

"You should leave the detecting to the detectives," Bruce said in a dismissive tone.

Jake looked affronted. "You'd like that, wouldn't you?"

Heather frowned at him. "What do you mean?"

"I know that you and your husband are thinking of opening a Bed and Breakfast in this very town, and you're here to do industrial espionage on Eden, and you went to the Bedshills' for the very same reason."

"I wouldn't exactly call it industrial espionage," Bruce began, and then let out a loud yell, bending under the table and clutching his shin. He looked at his wife. "Why did you kick me?"

"Shut your mouth, you silly fool," she snapped, drawing a collective gasp from the others at the table.

Bruce glared at her but didn't say any more.

"I can't speak for Mrs. Berkholder," Jonas said, "but I am sure that she welcomes *all* guests here. However, if you are here to spy on how Miriam runs this business in order to open your own establishment, I don't think that's the right thing to do. If you simply ask her, I'm sure she will be glad to assist you."

Miriam shot Jonas a grateful look. "Yes, I would be happy to help you. All you have to do is ask."

"I'm truly sorry," Bruce began, ignoring his wife's attempts to hush him. "We won't be in direct opposition to you, Mrs. Berkholder, because this is an Amish establishment, and ours of course won't be Amish."

Miriam nodded. So that was the Hansons' secret! They were intending to open a rival Bed and Breakfast business and were snooping around the established ones in the area. This meant that they weren't the jewelry thieves. That only left Jake, Kevin and Susan Smith, and Ava Douglas. Ava needed a hip replacement, and the thief had climbed up a drainpipe when robbing the jewelry store in town, so Miriam did not think it could be her.

Miriam now thought the thief was either Kevin Smith or Jake. After all, Miriam had caught Kevin looking in her kitchen cupboard, a cupboard under the very drawer where she had kept Tiffany's car keys, the keys to the car used in the robbery in town. Could his story about being hungry be believed?

CHAPTER 14

*M*iriam was a little tired after doing her grocery shopping. She loaded it into the buggy, and was about to drive home when she spied the little café across the road. She had been in there before, as one of the ladies in the community owned the quilt shop only one block away, and also as Miriam occasionally enjoyed a good cup of *kaffi* there after her grocery shopping.

Miriam needed to get back to the cleaning, but after all, Tiffany was back at Eden working, so she figured she could allow herself a short time to collect her thoughts. She used to relax when driving the buggy with her old horse, Henry, but she had given Henry to her *dochder*, Rachel, as she felt better with Rachel and her new *boppli* in a buggy pulled by an old, quiet horse.

Miriam's new horse was quiet enough, but he was young, and still inclined to be a little scared when cars passed too closely and roared their engines. She certainly could not relax while driving him. It wasn't that he was flighty, but he did startle upon occasion, even though he settled soon after. He was a typical young horse, but that did not do anything to help Miriam relax while driving him into town.

The only available table in the café was at the front, overlooking all the passers-by. Miriam usually sat at a table down the back, where she could watch everyone. She didn't like to sit in such a public position, but this time she had no option. She ordered coffee and a large piece of carrot cake. Miriam always considered that baked goods tasted nicer when she herself didn't have to make them.

Her thoughts at once turned to Jonas. He had hurried away last night and she had not had a chance to talk to him. She still had no idea what he wanted to talk to her about, but she figured it would all come out in time. Nevertheless, there was a niggling worry that settled in the pit of her stomach. Jonas certainly had something on his mind and she wanted to know what it was.

What if Jonas wanted to tell her he was going to marry someone else? Miriam's hands shook at the thought so she placed her coffee cup back on the table. *Nee*, it surely wasn't that. He had not shown even the slightest interest in any of the other women in the community. Another sudden thought struck Miriam. What if Jonas had been writing to a lady from another community? That sort of thing happened all the time. Yes, that made sense now. Jonas truly was going to tell her he intended to marry someone else.

Miriam dug her fingers into her palms to stop the tears that were threatening to fall. Jonas was in love with someone else. Why couldn't he have fallen in love with her?

Just then, a dark shadow fell over the table. Miriam looked up to see Timothy Yoder standing there. "May I join you?" he asked, but before he had even finished his sentence, he was sitting opposite her.

Miriam just wanted to be alone with her thoughts. She could hardly speak for fear that she might burst into tears.

Timothy did not even appear to notice that

Miriam was upset. "Have you thought over my proposal yet?" he asked her brusquely.

Miriam shook her head, and finally found her voice. "*Nee*, there is nothing to think over. I have given you my answer, and it won't change. I'm sorry Timothy, but I just can't marry you. I will *not* marry you."

Timothy's cheeks puffed out, and hard lines formed around the corners of his mouth. "I suggest you think about it." His tone was harsh.

Miriam by now was becoming quite annoyed. "No, Timothy. I don't mean to be rude, but you're upsetting me. I won't marry you, not now, not ever, so I must ask you to leave."

Timothy's jaw worked up and down, but he made no move to leave. Just then, another shadow fell over the table.

"Sorry I'm late, Miriam," Jonas said, casting a pointed look at Timothy's chair.

Timothy stood to his feet abruptly, almost knocking over the chair, and marched out of the café.

Jonas leaned across the table to Miriam. "I'm sorry to pretend I was here to meet you, Miriam, but I figured it was a peaceable way to get Timothy to leave. He looked quite angry. Did he upset you?

You look like you've been crying. Should you see the bishop about his behavior? Would you like me to speak to Timothy?"

Miriam shook her head. "It wasn't him so much. It's just that he caught me at a bad time, when I was worrying about…" Her voice trailed away. "Things," she added. "He asked me to marry him the other day and I said no, and he just now turned up to insist that I think it over. I told him again that I would never marry him, but he didn't want to take no for an answer. I'm afraid I might have been rude to him." Miriam sniffled into a tissue.

"I don't like to see you so upset," Jonas said.

Miriam attempted to smile at him. Now that she was upset, she figured it wouldn't matter too much if she was upset even more. "What was it that you were going to tell me the other day, Jonas?" She hoped he would just come straight out and tell her that he was going to marry someone else, as then she could move on with her life and do her best to get over him.

Jonas looked down at the table and shifted in his seat. "It's just that I was going to say, well, that is to say, um." He shot Miriam a brief look and then looked away again. "Do you mind me asking why you didn't want to marry Timothy Yoder?"

Miriam frowned at him. Did Jonas think she should have accepted Timothy's proposal? Was Jonas aware of her feelings for him and embarrassed by her feelings, given that he was going to marry someone else? Miriam shook her head to clear her thoughts. "Because I don't have any feelings for Timothy, obviously."

Was it her imagination, or did Jonas look pleased? "You don't?" he asked her.

"Of course not. I hope he doesn't trouble me anymore. I told him down by the pond that I wasn't interested, yet he persisted in asking me to think it over today."

Jonas shook his head. "If he troubles you any further, Miriam, please consider telling the bishop. So are you saying that you don't like Timothy as a husband, not that you never intend to marry?"

Miriam's brow puckered. "I'm not sure exactly what you mean."

Jonas shook his head again. "You don't have anything against getting married again, do you?"

Miriam shook her head. "*Nee*, I don't." *I would marry you in a heartbeat, Jonas*, she added silently.

Jonas bit his lip, and didn't say anything. After a

few moments, Miriam looked around the room at the other patrons. They were the only Amish people there, so no one would tease her about sitting with Jonas. Not that she minded being teased—it was all good-natured, but still, it always made her feel a little embarrassed. She looked back at Jonas to see he was fidgeting uncomfortably.

"Mary Stolfuz told me that you said you would never get married again," he suddenly blurted out, taking Miriam by surprise.

"Excuse me?" she said in shock. "What did you say, Jonas?" Surely she had misheard him.

Jonas's face flushed beet red. "I hope you don't mind me repeating what I heard," he said.

Miriam drummed her fingers on the table impatiently. "What exactly did you hear?"

Jonas spread out his hands on the table and stared at them. "Mary Stolfuz said that you would never get married again."

Miriam was taken aback. "Why ever would she say such a thing?"

Jonas shrugged. "She said you told her."

Miriam thought back. Mary Stolfuz was not a friend of hers, and she only knew her to say a passing *Hiya* at the meetings every second week. Could she have possibly said anything to give Mary that impression? Miriam was sure she hadn't. Aloud she said, "I really don't know Mary Stolfuz, and I'm sure I have never said such a thing to her, let alone to anyone else. She must be confusing me with someone else. Why, it's not even true."

An unmistakable look of relief passed over Jonas's face. "That's strange. She seemed absolutely certain, and she told me that more than once."

Miriam frowned. How could Mary make such a mistake? Unless it wasn't a mistake, and Mary had told Jonas that for her own reasons. But what reasons could she have? Mary was married, so it wasn't as if she wanted Jonas for herself. Miriam thought on it some more, and then something dawned on her. "Jonas, isn't Mary Timothy Yoder's *schweschder*?"

Jonas was silent for a moment, and then nodded slowly. "*Jah*."

So that was it. Miriam was no longer puzzled as to why Mary would tell Jonas such a fanciful story. She realized that Mary said it to help Timothy's chances, but surely that meant that Mary thought Jonas was interested in her, Miriam? Why else would Mary say such a thing, if not to stop any interest Jonas had in Miriam?

Miriam rubbed her temples in an attempt to

forestall the throbbing headache that was forming. None of this made any sense. She shot a look at Jonas, but he was no help, squirming uncomfortably in his seat.

Miriam sighed and looked away, and then gasped when she saw the person on the other side of the room.

CHAPTER 15

"Jonas, look at that!"

Jonas spun around and he, too, gasped with surprise.

There, sitting at the very back of the café, was Kevin Smith. He was stuffing a burger into his mouth, and he had another burger on his plate, along with a side serve of the biggest plate of fries Miriam had ever seen. After he consumed that burger, he drank the whole contents of a very large soda before turning to the other burger.

"That poor man looks absolutely starving," Miriam said with surprise. "I was sure I provided him with plenty of food at Eden."

"Perhaps he has an eating disorder," Jonas

offered. "I have heard that *Englischers* do suffer from eating disorders from time to time."

Miriam nodded. "I have never seen anyone eat so much and so fast, either." She averted her eyes, feeling bad for staring. "Still, it is none of my business," she added.

"Perhaps that's why he's been acting suspiciously," Jonas said. "I suspected Kevin of being the jewelry thief, but now I wonder if he was acting suspiciously simply because he wanted more food."

Miriam shot another look at the man. "Yes, and I've noticed that Susan scolds him when she thinks he's eating too much."

At that point, Kevin must have noticed them watching, because he beckoned them over. Miriam and Jonas walked over to his table. "Won't you join me?" he asked. "That is, unless I've disturbed your meal?"

Miriam shook her head. "I only came here for some coffee, but I've finished it, and Jonas happened to see me when passing. We were both about to leave."

Kevin wrung his hands. "Would you mind not mentioning to my wife that you saw me here?" he said. "I mean, I know you Amish don't lie or anything, but please don't volunteer the information to her, if you would?"

Miriam and Jonas assured him that they wouldn't.

"Susan has me on a strict diet," Kevin said. "She's worried about my cholesterol. Not that it's high or anything," he said, waving a hand dismissively, but then he frowned. "Well, it wasn't before, but it probably is now. I've been binge eating, because she won't let me eat a normal sized meal. She watches everything I eat, and then she scolds me. She doesn't eat much, and I don't think she realizes how much men actually eat. I've been absolutely ravenous, I tell you!"

He broke off when a waitress appeared at his table. Miriam and Jonas both said they didn't want to order anything, but Kevin ordered a spiced pumpkin latte and a slice of apple pie.

"I hope you don't think I'm terrible," he said when he had finished his food. "I've been starving, so hungry that I can't even think straight. Susan wants me to live on lettuce leaves. I'm going to order a whole pie to go."

With that, he picked up his large backpack from

the floor. Miriam and Jonas exchanged glances. They had previously suspected that his backpack contained stolen jewelry. He showed them the contents of the backpack.

Miriam looked inside. It contained several cans of soda, and all manner of candy. "So *that's* what you were doing in my kitchen the other day," Miriam said. "You were looking for food."

A look of confusion flickered over Kevin's face. "Yes, I told you that. What did you think I was doing?" He was silent for a few more moments, before saying, "Oh, did you think I was the jewelry thief?" He burst into laughter. "I'm actually a lawyer."

Miriam considered that being a lawyer didn't prevent someone from being a jewelry thief, but she merely smiled and nodded. Tiffany had said that Susan's engagement ring might not be stolen after all. Kevin continued to laugh.

"Do you have any idea who the jewelry thief could be?" Jonas asked him.

Kevin stopped laughing. "As a matter of fact, I don't. I can see why the two of you were suspicious, though. It seems like it would have to be one of the guests, and that doesn't leave many options."

"It surely has to be one of the guests," Jonas

pointed out. "The keys to Tiffany's car were stolen right from Miriam's kitchen, and then there was your engagement ring."

Kevin flushed beet red. "I don't actually know if that engagement ring *was* stolen," he said.

Miriam was puzzled. "What do you mean?" she asked him.

He hesitated a long time before answering. "Susan and I had a big argument over my eating, and she took off her engagement ring and threw it at me. In fact, we've had a lot of arguments over my eating in the short time since we got married. Then she went to take a bath." He stopped speaking and held up both his hands. "I know you're thinking she shouldn't have lied to the sheriff, but she was so upset, that I don't think she actually was lying. I think she forgets taking off her ring and throwing it at me and she really thinks she left it in the room."

Miriam didn't see how that could be the case, but she simply nodded.

"Have you told the sheriff?" Jonas asked him.

Kevin hurried to reassure them. "Yes, I called the sheriff from my cell phone as soon as I could and told him the situation. I apologize that I didn't tell you, but I was so embarrassed."

Jonas frowned deeply. "If the ring wasn't stolen,

then it means that the jewelry thief might not be one of the guests. Now the only connection to Eden is that someone stole the key and then took Tiffany's car."

"It *is* strange that whoever it was returned Tiffany's car," Miriam supplied.

Jonas and Kevin both agreed. "It is a very puzzling situation," Jonas said.

"And if the engagement ring has merely fallen down behind a floorboard—and mind you, I've checked," Kevin said, "then there has been only one robbery. It's strange that there was one small jewelry robbery in town, but the thief stole Miss Tiffany's car to commit the crime. What's more, it's the only jewelry robbery that's been reported."

Jonas nodded. "None of it makes any sense, but hopefully the sheriff will soon throw some light onto the situation. Meanwhile, with Miriam's permission, I can have a thorough look for the engagement ring, perhaps by taking up a floorboard and then replacing it as good as new."

"Of course." Miriam smiled at him. "I hope Jonas can find your engagement ring for you, Kevin." Miriam, however, was deep in thought. Did this mean she should no longer suspect the guests?

But why would someone steal a key from Eden and drive Tiffany's car to town simply to commit one small robbery?

CHAPTER 16

$\mathcal{M}$iriam drove her buggy home, having more questions than answers. Why would Mary Stolfuz say such a thing to Jonas? Did Mary think Jonas was interested in Miriam, knowing that her brother, Timothy, was about to ask Miriam to marry him? And what did Jonas think about her? Was she simply a friend, or did he see her as more than a friend?

And then there was the matter of the jewelry theft. Miriam did not know about such matters, but even she thought it strange that there had been one small robbery and the thief had not struck again. And why steal a key from Eden to drive the car into town to rob a jewelry store?

Miriam was so preoccupied that she stopped watching her horse's ears for a moment. Usually, her horse's ears pointed to the direction in which he would shy, so she was usually able to divert his attention by gently jiggling the reins or speaking to him. This time, however, Miriam was distracted.

A plover darted up from the bushes right in front of the horse's face. The horse shied violently and then broke into a gallop. Miriam was thankful for her fast reflexes, because she managed to stop the horse. Still, even when the horse was at a standstill, he was shaking and had broken into a lather of sweat. Miriam got down from the buggy, keeping a careful hold on the reins, and walked to the horse to reassure him. She stroked his neck and spoke to him calmly.

Miriam was standing right next to the pond, and wanted to go around the horse and stand on higher ground, but she wanted to wait until he was calm. She didn't want to risk the horse taking fright again just as she was standing in front of him, and he was still trembling.

Just as Miriam thought the horse was calming down, a flash of yellow ran between the horse's legs.

The horse took off, bumping into Miriam and

sending her flying backward into the pond. She fell heavily, and threw out her wrist to save herself.

The pond was shallow in that part, but Miriam was soaked from head to toe. Tears pricked her eyes as a sharp pain shot through her wrist, as if someone had stuck a red hot poker into it every time she moved it.

Miriam pulled herself from the pond with her good arm and then sat on the bank. She felt awfully sorry for herself and it was all she could do not to burst into tears. Just then, Cuddles appeared and stared at her, his bottom teeth protruding.

"Was that you?" Miriam addressed the little dog. "I'll have you know that you frightened my horse, and you've probably broken my wrist."

The little dog walked over and licked Miriam's shoe. She could not help but laugh at the comical expression on his face. "Where's your owner?" she asked him. "I hope she's nearby, because I'm in a lot of pain, and I don't think I can walk far."

Cuddles ignored her, his attention taken by the family of ducks on the pond. He barked at them. When he finished barking, Miriam called out, "Ava? Mrs. Douglas? It's Miriam. I've hurt myself!"

There was no response. Miriam called out five

times, but there was still no response. She decided to walk the short distance to the road, but her wrist hurt with every step, and now her shoulder was hurting, too. The little dog followed her.

Miriam knew that her horse would head for home, and someone would come looking for her, so she leaned against a tree for support. Finally, she heard a horse coming her way fast. Miriam breathed a long sigh of relief. She was even more relieved to see it was Jonas's buggy.

Jonas jumped from his buggy and ran over to her. "Miriam, are you hurt?"

"*Jah.* Is my horse all right?"

Jonas nodded. "He was in a terrible lather of sweat, and Ethan is washing him down. What happened?"

Miriam pointed with her good hand to the little dog sitting behind her. "Cuddles scared him. Well, he was already scared by a plover and tried to bolt, so I stopped him. He was still trembling, so I got out of the buggy to talk to him to calm him down. He was only just calm when Cuddles appeared from nowhere and ran between his legs, startling him again. He knocked me back into the pond."

"Miriam, are you hurt?" Jonas asked again urgently.

Miriam could hardly speak. She felt as though she was about to cry, now that she was safe, and that Jonas had come to rescue her. "I'm sore, and my shoulder hurts, but I'm afraid I've broken my wrist." With that, she burst into a flood of tears, much to her embarrassment.

Jonas put his arm around her and helped her into his buggy. He put a blanket around her shoulders, and another blanket across her knees. He scooped up Cuddles and put him in the buggy, too, and then set off in the direction of town.

"Where are we going?" Miriam asked.

"To the *doktor*," Jonas said.

Miriam made to protest, but she was worried that her wrist was broken. "*Denki*, Jonas." She looked over at Jonas, and noticed for the first time that he was as white as a sheet. "Jonas, are you ill?"

Jonas shot her a look. "What do you mean?"

"Your face has gone pale."

Jonas looked straight ahead. "You gave me the most terrible fright, Miriam," he said in a small voice. "All these terrible images went through my head when I saw your horse galloping up to Eden and no sign of you. Why, I imagined…" His voice trailed away. "Miriam, I'd like to swap buggy horses with you for a while until your horse is more experienced," he said in a stronger voice.

"*Denki*, Jonas, and *denki* for rescuing me."

Jonas turned to her. "I'll always rescue you, Miriam."

CHAPTER 17

The doctor told Miriam that her wrist was not broken, but was sprained. He warned her that sprains can sometimes be more painful than simple breaks.

After Miriam took the painkillers given to her by the doctor, her wrist was hurting considerably less, but her shoulder still hurt. The doctor had told her she would be sore for around a week, and to take it easy. Of course, it was impossible for Miriam to take things easy as she had a Bed and Breakfast to run. Still, she considered she would feel much better after she took a long, hot bath. She would then apply arnica liniment to all her bruises.

Jonas had called Eden from the doctor's office to tell Tiffany what had happened to Miriam, and to tell Ava not to worry about her dog as he had Cuddles with him.

Jonas had barely spoken to Miriam on the whole trip back to Eden from the doctor's office, and she wondered why.

When she arrived at Eden, both Tiffany and Ava Douglas were waiting for her. Ava flung her arms around Miriam's neck and burst into tears. "It's all my fault," she wailed. "You could have been killed. It's all my fault."

Tiffany managed to remove Ava's arms from Miriam's neck. "Come on, I'll make you a nice cup of hot meadow tea," she said to Ava. "I'm sure Miriam needs to get into some dry clothes."

"Yes, I do," Miriam said over her shoulder as she headed straight for her bathroom. Miriam smiled to herself about the way in which Tiffany had taken over the situation. She was certainly proving to be a good helper.

Miriam intended to lie in the bath for ages, but she wasn't one to be idle. Also, her wrist was tightly bandaged, and given that she didn't want to get the bandages wet, she wasn't as comfortable as she had expected to be in the bath.

She dried herself and managed to dress herself, then hurried down to the kitchen, thinking she too could do with a nice hot cup of meadow tea. She took her seat at the kitchen table and Tiffany placed the meadow tea in front of her. She shot her a grateful look, but was dismayed to see that Ava was still crying.

"It wasn't Cuddles' fault," Miriam said, trying to reassure the woman. "My horse was already upset by a plover, so Cuddles' appearance was the last straw."

"I know it wasn't Cuddles' fault," Ava wailed. "It was my fault! If I hadn't done any of this, Cuddles wouldn't have been with me down by the pond. Why, what if you had been killed? I just can't bear to think about it. It's all my fault," she said again for the umpteenth time.

Jonas stuck his head around the door. "How are you feeling now, Miriam?"

Miriam gestured to the chair opposite her with her un-bandaged arm. "I feel much better now, Jonas, *denki*. Please join us for some meadow tea."

Jonas looked hesitant, but took a seat, nevertheless. Tiffany poured him a cup of meadow tea, and then cut a large wet-bottom shoo fly pie into pieces. Miriam accepted the plate of pie from Tiffany, and tucked into it, savoring the molasses and brown sugar. Being knocked into a pond by a horse and spraining her wrist had certainly made her hungry.

Ava ate a piece of pie, but only moments later, burst into a fresh flood of tears. "I did it!" she said. "I'm going to jail, but I have to tell you the truth. It's all my fault."

Miriam frowned. "Of course you're not going to jail, Ava. It was an accident."

Ava shook her head. "You don't understand. Cuddles could have gotten you killed, and he was only by the pond because I was by the pond."

"It's not a crime to be down by the pond," Jonas said in bewilderment. "It was just an accident."

Ava shook her head. "I'm the jewelry thief," she suddenly blurted out.

Everyone gasped. Miriam looked at her in disbelief.

"I stole the diamond necklace from the jewelry store. I had it hidden in a bag down by the pond, and I was going to return it the night before I left Eden."

Miriam wondered if the painkillers were affecting her mind. Surely Ava hadn't said what she thought she had said? It seemed altogether too strange.

"Let me get this straight," Jonas said. "You're the one who stole the diamond necklace?"

Ava nodded vigorously. "Yes, that's right. I did it."

"And your conscience got the better of you, so you planned to return it?" Jonas asked.

Ava shook her head. "Yes and no. I mean, yes, I was going to return it, but no, not because of my conscience. I always intended to return it. I stole it with the intention of returning it."

Miriam leaned forward and put her head in her hands. She'd had a trying day, and Ava's explanation wasn't making it any easier.

"Maybe you should explain it to us right from the beginning," Jonas said helpfully. Miriam shot him a grateful glance.

Ava sighed and wrung her hands. "I was lying about needing a hip replacement," she said with a shamefaced expression. "I'm sorry about that. I was the one who climbed up the drainpipe."

Miriam nodded. Finally, something made sense. "But why did you steal it with the intention of giving it back?" she asked Ava.

Ava spread her fingers out over the table and sighed again. "It's the fifth anniversary of my dear husband's death. I wanted to do something to celebrate his memory. Oh, I should explain, he was a famous international jewel thief. That was back in his youth, of course. And I suppose some would say he was infamous, rather than famous." She waved her hands expansively. "He used to tell me all his exploits, and it sounded so much fun. I always wondered if I could do it. I'm a yoga instructor, so I have the agility, and I was a champion gymnast when I was young. I pretended I'd need a hip replacement as a cover story."

Tiffany nodded. "Aha! A cover story."

"So you robbed the jewelry store to see if you could do what your husband did?" Miriam asked in disbelief.

Ava leaned across and patted Miriam's hand. "That's right, dear. It's rather annoying how most people treat elderly people. Why, only a month or two ago, I was thinking of selling my house and buying another house, and all the realtor could talk about was how it would be a good asset for me to leave to my children. Would he say that to someone who was younger? No, he wouldn't! I wanted to prove I could do something, all by myself, even at my age."

Ava kept talking, while Miriam tried to process the information. She hadn't suspected Ava, not at all. Miriam looked up when Jonas spoke. "And you said you weren't going to keep the necklace?"

Ava looked affronted. "Of course not! I'm not a thief. I was only borrowing it, to prove to myself I could do it. That's why I only took one item, and not a valuable item at that. I just didn't realize all the trouble it would cause. I'm so sorry," she said to Miriam, patting her hand once more. "I didn't think it through. It was so silly of me. I didn't realize that other people here would be under suspicion, and then because I was down at the pond, my little dog nearly got you killed."

"I'm fine, Ava," Miriam said, looking at Jonas. She raised her eyebrows in a silent question. What should they do about Ava? Should they tell the sheriff?

"Now I'm going to go to jail," Ava wailed. "Who will look after Cuddles?"

The little dog looked at Miriam.

Jonas abruptly stood to his feet. "I need to speak privately to Miriam. Ava and Tiffany, would you mind if we left, please?"

CHAPTER 18

"*M*iriam," he repeated, and her heart skipped a beat at the sound of her name. "I need to say this before there are any more interruptions."

"I know what you're going to say," Miriam said, looking at the pond where Jonas had taken her.

Jonas raised one eyebrow. "You do?"

"*Jah.*"

"And you don't mind?"

Miriam shook her head. "*Nee*, it's not up to me to judge. *De Herr* is the only judge."

Jonas frowned. He even looked handsome when he was stern, Miriam thought.

"I don't understand what you mean," he said.

Miriam smiled. It wasn't a happy smile, but a resigned smile. "Ava, of course. You're going to say that you don't want to tell the sheriff that she stole the diamond necklace."

Jonas's face fell. "That's not what I was going to say, but I will take the diamond necklace back to the sheriff and ask him to go easy on Ava. I'll explain the whole story."

Miriam thought that was very kind of Jonas. "You don't think she will go to jail, do you?" she said.

"I'm sure the sheriff will be understanding, given the circumstances." He walked over to Miriam and took her un-bandaged hand. The feel of his large, rough paw around her small hand made her blush. "Miriam, I said I need to say this before there's yet another interruption, and I meant it. I've decided just to come straight out and say it, and if you don't like what I have to say, then I hope we can still be friends." A blush crept over his face.

Miriam frowned. "But we'll always be friends, Jonas."

Whatever could he say that would be so bad? An uneasy feeling lodged itself in the pit of her stomach, and not even her hand pressing against the nape of her neck brought relief.

"Miriam," said Jonas, "I'm in love with you." Miriam gasped, but Jonas continued. "I know you always say we're friends, and you probably don't want to ruin our friendship, but I've been in love with you since the first time I saw you. I've wanted to tell you lately, but I was afraid how you would react."

"I don't know what to say."

Jonas took a sharp breath in, and then he said, "Say you will be my wife."

The air was knocked from Miriam. She took a step back and almost landed in the pond, but Jonas was there to steady her footing.

"What if I say yes?" she answered more to herself than to Jonas.

"Then I would truly be blessed."

"Oh, Jonas," she whispered, "I am the one who is blessed. Yes. Yes. My answer is yes."

"Do you really mean that?"

"Yes."

Now it was Jonas who took a step back and nearly fell in the pond. After Miriam helped to steady his footing, they stood together and listened to the lapping water. To think, Miriam had thought she would never have the love of a good man again for the rest of her life, and now, among the ducks and the whispering reeds, and she had become engaged to a man she dearly loved instead.

ABOUT RUTH HARTZLER

USA Today best-selling author, Ruth Hartzler, was a college professor of Biblical history and ancient languages. Now she writes faith-based romances, cozy mysteries, and archeological adventures.

Ruth Hartzler is best known for her Amish romances, which were inspired by her Anabaptist upbringing. When Ruth is not writing, she spends her time walking her dog and baking cakes for her adult children, all of whom have food allergies. Ruth also enjoys correcting grammar on shop signs when nobody is looking.

www.ruthhartzler.com